STORY CARNIVAL

THE PROSE AND POETRY SERIES

FLOY WINKS DeLANCEY
WILLIAM J. IVERSON

STORY
CARNIVAL

THE L. W. SINGER COMPANY

SYRACUSE   CHICAGO

The Authors

FLOY WINKS DeLANCEY

Associate Professor of English,
State University of New York, Teachers College at Brockport

WILLIAM J. IVERSON

Professor of Education and Specialist in Reading,
Stanford University

Book Design by

STEFAN SALTER

Illustrations by

GUY BROWN WISER ASSOCIATES

Richard Foes, Claude Leet, Ken Smith

860.1   *11133*

CONTENTS

UNIT ONE BOYS AND GIRLS LIKE YOU AND ME

UNIT TWO ANIMAL FRIENDS

UNIT THREE MERRY TALES

UNIT FOUR CHILDREN'S THEATER

UNIT FIVE   HOLIDAYS ARE FUN

UNIT SIX   LONG AGO AND FAR AWAY

BOYS AND GIRLS
LIKE YOU AND ME

THE BOTTLE

THAT WENT TO SEA

Lilian Moore

One day Tommy's mother got a letter. She read the letter to Tommy.

This is what the letter said:

Dear Mrs. Jones,

Yes, you may have the little brown house on Little White Beach. You may live in it all summer.

"All summer!" said Tommy. "Will we live at a beach all summer?"

"Yes," said his mother, and you could see she was happy, too.

"When will we go?" asked Tommy. He did not see how he could wait.

"Soon," said his mother.

Soon? How many days was that? It seemed a long, long time to Tommy.

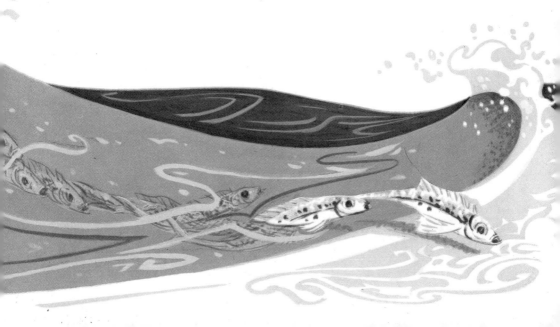

Then one day his mother and father began to pack. Tommy helped, too. They packed boxes and bags. Bags and boxes. They all went into the car.

And off went Tommy and his mother and father to the little brown house on the beach.

As soon as they got there, Tommy ran out to play. He played in the sand. He found shells. He found a starfish. He splashed in the water.

"Oh, I like it here!" he said. "I like it here on Little White Beach."

He played the next day, too. He played in the sand. He splashed in the water. He found more shells, and another starfish.

He played the day after that, and the day after that. Then he looked around. He looked at the sea. He looked at the sand.

But Tommy did not feel happy.

He ran back to the little brown house.

"Mother," he said, "there's no one to play with here."

"There will be soon," said his mother. "We came here a little early. There will be other children here soon."

Soon? How many days was that? Soon always sounded as if it would be right away. But it often seemed like a long, long time.

Tommy walked slowly out to the beach.

He wanted to dig a deep, deep hole and fill it with water. But it was no fun to do it alone.

He wanted to build a big, big, BIG sand castle. But it was hard to do it alone.

He stood and looked at the sea.

13

All at once, Tommy saw something bobbing around in the water.

It came closer and closer.

Tommy pulled it in. It was a bottle, a little green bottle with a cork in it.

A bottle floating in from the sea!

Tommy thought about a story he once heard. In the story, a man on a big boat threw a bottle into the sea.

There was a letter in the bottle.

The bottle sailed far away with the letter.

Tommy ran into the house. "Mother," he said, "I am going to write a letter to put in this bottle."

This is what the letter said:

14

To the one who finds this bottle. My name is Tommy Jones. I am 8 years old. I live on Little White Beach in a little brown house.

Then Tommy, put the letter into the bottle, and pushed the cork back in. He ran down to the beach with the bottle, and threw it as far as he could, far into the sea.

"Have a good trip!" Tommy laughed, as he watched the bottle float away, out with the sea.

"Maybe it will be picked up by a big liner at sea!" thought Tommy.

Maybe someone far out on a fishing boat would pick it up and read the letter. Maybe someone in a tugboat out at sea would find it first.

Maybe it would sail on and on till it went all around the world!

Tommy watched his bottle till he could not see it any more.

The little bottle did sail away as the sea went out.

But that night, when the sea came in again, it carried the bottle back to the beach. Not to Little White Beach, but to another little beach not far away, called Sandy Shore.

The next morning a boy was walking along the beach at Sandy Shore.

16

He picked up the little green bottle and saw there was a letter inside.

He ran to his house.

"Mother," he said, "look, there's a letter inside this bottle! Let's read it!"

They read the letter:

> To the one who finds this bottle:
> My name is Tommy Jones. I am eight years old. I live on Little White Beach in a little brown house.

"Hooray!" cried the boy. "Hooray! At last there's a boy around here I can play with!"

Then he said, "Mother, may I go over to Little White Beach? I know where the little brown house is."

"Why, yes," said his mother. "It's not very far. And ask Tommy Jones if he wants to come and play here, too."

Off ran the boy with the little green bottle, off to the Little White Beach.

Tommy was playing in the sand. He was wishing again that he could make a big, big sand castle.

"Hi!" said someone behind him.

Tommy looked around.

There was a boy looking at him. "Hi!" said the boy again. "I found your bottle with the

18

letter in it!" He held out the bottle to Tommy.

"You did?" cried Tommy. "Where did you find it?"

"Right down there," said the boy, and he showed Tommy. "Right at the next beach where I live. I came over to play."

Tommy laughed.

So his bottle had not gone far away. No big liner had picked it up. No man on a fishing boat had seen it. No tugboat out at sea had found it. No one across the world had read his letter.

19

Better than all that — another boy he could play with had found it!

"How would you like to build a sand castle?" he asked his friend.

And they began to build a big, big, BIG sand castle — the kind that only two boys can make when they build together.

WHAT HAPPENED?

Tommy had fun at first playing on the beach. Then he wanted someone to play with. He found a bottle. What did he do with the bottle?

Tommy found someone to play with. How did he find a playmate?

THINK IT OVER

Tommy's mother said they would go to Little White Beach soon. Tommy thought the time would never come. Does time ever pass slowly for you? When?

Tommy was lonesome at the beach. He wanted someone to play with. What games do you play when you are by yourself? How can you make new friends when you move into a new house?

Tommy wrote a letter. He did not know who would get the letter. How do you begin a letter when you know who is going to get it?

20

POOR JIMMY SMITH

Eda and Richard Crist

Poor Jimmy Smith. He was eating some popcorn and he bit his thumb.

His mother wrapped it up and then he went out to play. On the sidewalk he met Betty Jane Jones who lived next door.

"Hello, Jimmy," said Betty Jane. "What happened to your thumb?"

Jimmy was ashamed to tell her he bit it himself. So he said, "A tiger scratched it."

Reprinted by permission of the authors.

"Tigers are in the zoo," said Betty Jane. "And you didn't go there today."

"This one escaped," said Jimmy.

Poor Jimmy Smith. He never should have said that. But he did.

Betty Jane Jones cried, "Oooh!" and ran into her house. "Mother! Mother!" she called. "A big wild tiger's escaped from the zoo!"

"Are you sure?" her mother asked.

"Yes, I'm sure," Betty Jane said. "Because Jimmy Smith told me so. It even scratched his thumb."

"Oh, dear!" said her mother. "Lock all the doors while I call the zoo!"

At the zoo, the head zoo-keeper answered the phone. "Hello," he said. "This is the head zoo-keeper speaking . . .

22

Yes, Mrs. Jones . . . What? . . .
Escaped tiger? . . . Oh, my
g-goodness! I'll look right away!"

The head zoo-keeper shouted
for his two helper zoo-keepers
and they ran to the tiger cage.
They all counted tigers to see if
one was missing — "One, two,
three, four, five, six."

"Didn't we have seven?" asked
the first helper.

"No," said the head zoo-keeper.
"We only had six — I *think*."

"*I* think we had seven," said
the second helper.

"Or perhaps," said the first helper, "it was six."

"I'll look in their den," said the head zoo-keeper. "Maybe, if we had seven, one is taking a nap in there." He opened the door and looked in the den.

"Oh, my!" he exclaimed. "The den is empty!"

"Then," said the first helper, "if we had six tigers, they're all still here."

"But," said the second helper, "if we had seven, then one has escaped!"

"Maybe one *has* escaped!" said all the zoo-keepers, looking at each other.

"Quick!" shouted the head zoo-keeper. "Get out the escaped-animal truck!"

In a few minutes the escaped-animal truck raced down the street. It stopped beside a policeman.

"Have you seen an escaped tiger?" the zoo-keepers asked.

The policeman yawned. "Not today."

"A yellow one," said the head keeper.

24

"With black stripes," said the first helper.

"And a tail," said the second helper.

"Black stripes?" said the policeman. "You sure it wasn't a zebra? Zebras have stripes. Tails too, I believe."

"Not yellow ones," said the head zoo-keeper.

"Never saw a yellow zebra," said the policeman. "You sure it wasn't a tiger? Tigers are yellow. They have stripes too, I believe."

"It *was* a tiger," said all the zoo-keepers.

"My sakes!" said the policeman. "A *tiger*! I'll have to warn everybody to get off the streets! I must get the other policemen to help look for him. I'll get the Boy Scouts!" With this, he jumped onto his motorcycle and roared down the street.

The policeman told all the other policemen to jump on their motorcycles and to start looking for the tiger. He told the fire department to start looking. He told the Boy Scouts to start looking. He told everybody he saw to go home and lock

their doors and he told all the stores to close.

Around and around the town raced the zoo-keeper truck with the keepers.

Around and around the town roared the policemen on their motorcycles.

Around and around the town thundered the fire engine, its siren screaming.

Around and around the town ran the Boy Scouts, searching backyards and alleys for the tiger.

While all this was happening, the six tigers, left alone in the zoo, discovered something. They discovered that the door of their den was open! The head zoo-keeper had forgotten to close it.

So they walked out.

They walked right out of the zoo.

They rolled and tumbled in the grass for awhile. Then they went into town.

They walked slowly along Main Street, looking at things in the store windows.

Suddenly a Boy Scout saw them. He ran around the corner and shouted to a policeman. The policeman roared off on his motorcycle. He shouted to the fire-engine driver. The fire-engine driver thundered off to find the escaped-animal truck.

Soon the six tigers were running for their lives with everybody after them. They ran down Main Street and up Maple Street and down Union Street and up Washington Street and down Plumwiddie Street and up Pineapple Street. Then they ran down East Bubbleston Street. That was where Jimmy Smith lived.

Poor Jimmy Smith. He was standing on the sidewalk, eating popcorn with his left hand, when the tigers came.

The first tiger knocked him down and kept on going.

The five other tigers went *thumpity-thumpity-thumpity-thump* along his back and kept on going.

Then Jimmy looked up. He saw ten motorcycle policemen stop the tigers. He saw twenty-one Scouts catch them with ropes. He saw thirteen firemen tie them to a tree. And then he saw the escaped-animal truck whizz around the corner.

The truck stopped. The three zoo-keepers jumped out. "Six escaped tigers!" they cried, looking at each other.

"And there are six more back in the zoo!" exclaimed the first helper.

"That means," said the second helper, counting

on his fingers, "that we have *twelve* tigers all together!"

"Are you sure?" The head zoo-keeper began to count the helper's fingers.

"Six there and six here makes twelve everywhere," said the helper. "And please count on your own fingers."

"Oh, excuse me," said the head zoo-keeper. He frowned. "Well, we can't stand here counting tigers all day. Into the truck with them!"

Everybody helped to push the tigers into the truck. Then off it raced to the zoo. The policemen went back to work. The firemen went back to the fire station. The Scouts went home and Jimmy Smith got up off the sidewalk.

"Hello, Jimmy," said Betty Jane Jones, who had come out of her house. "What are those marks on your shirt?"

"They're tiger tracks," said Jimmy.

"Ooooh!" said Betty Jane. "And what happened to your other thumb — the one that isn't wrapped up?"

Jimmy looked at his other thumb. He was surprised. "It — it looks as if a tiger has scratched it," he said.

Poor Jimmy Smith! This time he was telling the truth!

WHAT HAPPENED?

Jimmy Smith said a tiger had scratched his thumb. What really had happened to his thumb? Why did he tell Betty Jane that a tiger had scratched it?

Betty Jane told her mother that a tiger had escaped from the zoo. Mrs. Jones called the zoo. She told them that a tiger had escaped. What did the head zoo-keeper do? The people at the zoo could not decide how many tigers they had. Of course this is a pretend part of the story.

The zoo people went to look for the escaped tiger. What did the six tigers at the zoo discover then? What did they do?

Poor Jimmy Smith! His finger really was scratched by a tiger later on. How did this happen?

SOMETHING BETTER

David McCord

We have a nice clean new green lawn,
And that's the one I'm playing on.
But down the street a little piece
There is a man who has three geese.
And when you see them, just beyond
You'll see a nice new deep blue pond.

DANNY'S WISH COMES TRUE

Clyde Robert Bulla

Danny Hopper lived in the top of a big apartment house. From his window he could see the city street far below. Sometimes he saw a dog. Sometimes a fire engine went by. But most of the time there was nothing new for him to see.

He had no yard to play in. When school was out, he had no one to play with. His mother had a cat named Jill, but Jill didn't like to play. All she did was eat and wash herself and sleep.

So Danny made up a game that he could play by himself. He called it the cowboy game.

From *Surprise for a Cowboy* by Clyde Robert Bulla. Copyright, 1950, by Clyde Robert Bulla. Reprinted by permission of the publisher, Thomas Y. Crowell Company.

He had a chair that he called his horse. He rode it up and down. He called his bedroom the corral and he played he was driving cattle into it. He had a piece of rope, and he could rope a calf with it. The calf was his father's footstool.

A long time ago Danny's father had been a cowboy. Now Danny wanted to be a cowboy, too.

One night Mother was reading a book. Father was reading a paper, with his feet on the footstool. Danny was riding up and down on his chair.

"Get up, pony," he said. "We'll catch that calf!"

He threw his rope. It fell over his father's feet.

"Here!" Father laughed and took the rope off his feet. "What are you doing?"

"I'm playing the cowboy game," said Danny.

"He plays it all day long," said Mother.

"I like to play cowboy." Danny sat down on the footstool by Father's chair. "Will you tell me about the ranch where you lived when you were a boy?"

"Don't you ever get tired of hearing about that?" asked Father.

"No," said Danny. "I like to hear about the ranch house and the horses and the cattle. Wasn't it fun to live on a ranch?"

"Yes," said Father. "We worked hard, but we had fun, too. My brother and I rode together and went to the roundups together. You know who my brother is, don't you?"

"He is my Uncle Mack," said Danny.

34

"Yes," said Father, "and now he has a big ranch of his own."

"I wish I could see a real ranch," said Danny.

Father and Mother looked at each other. Danny knew by the way they looked that they had a secret. "What is the secret?" he asked them.

"If we told you," said Mother, "it wouldn't be a secret."

"Will it be a big surprise?" asked Danny.

"Wait and see," said Father.

Danny waited. He waited a week and nothing happened.

Then one night there was a knock at the door.

Danny opened the door. A man came in. He was a tall man, and he looked a little like Father. His clothes were like the ones that Father wore,

35

but his shoes were different. The tall man wore cowboy boots.

"It's Uncle Mack!" cried Danny.

"Hello, Danny! Hello, everybody!" said Uncle Mack.

Mother and Father shook hands with him. Jill, the cat, came out of her box to see who was there. Everybody talked at once.

"I've been on the road all day," said Uncle Mack. "Is there anything for a hungry man to eat?"

They all went into the kitchen.

"I hope you can stay a long time," said Danny.

"I can't stay long," said Uncle Mack. "I have to get back to my ranch. Are you going with me?"

"Me?" Danny looked at Mother and Father. "May I go with Uncle Mack? May I really?"

"Do you want to go?" asked Mother.

"Yes," said Danny. "Yes, yes!"

"Good!" said Uncle Mack. "That's what I came for. I came to take you home with me for the summer."

"And this is the surprise!" said Danny.

"Do you like it?" asked Uncle Mack.

"It's the best surprise I ever had. I'm going to be a cowboy!" Danny jumped up and down. He made so much noise that Jill, the cat, laid back her ears and ran. She hid so far under the table that only her tail stuck out.

Early one morning Danny and Uncle Mack started for the ranch. When they got into the car, Danny looked out. He saw Mother and Father at their window high in the apartment house. They waved, and he waved back. Then he and Uncle Mack were on their way.

All day they rode along. They passed farms. They crossed rivers. They stayed all night in a town.

The next day they came to the mountains.

"Are we nearly there?" asked Danny.

"Not yet," said Uncle Mack. "Look for a mountain with a flat top. When you see that, you will know we are nearly there."

37

Danny looked for a flat-topped mountain. He looked and looked, and after a while he almost forgot it. Then, all at once, he saw it. It was a long, low mountain with a top that looked as flat as a floor.

"I see the flat-topped mountain!" he said.

"And here is the ranch," said Uncle Mack.

They turned in at a gate. Over the gate was a sign: "Bar-K Ranch."

They drove across a pasture. At the end of a long, bumpy road, Danny saw a white house with a red roof.

A woman came out of the house.

"Here is your Aunt Betty," said Uncle Mack.

Danny called to her, "Hello, Aunt Betty!"

"Hello, Danny!" she called back. "Welcome to Bar-K Ranch."

A collie dog came running around the house.

"Here is Shep," said Uncle Mack. "He wants to say hello. Shake hands with Danny, Shep."

The dog barked and held out his paw. Danny shook hands with him.

"Shep is glad to see you," said Aunt Betty, "and so am I."

Uncle Mack put the car away. Danny went into the house with Aunt Betty.

He liked the house. It was big and cool. There was one room with a deer's head on the wall. There were old guns on the wall, too, and there was a stone fireplace.

There was a room with nothing in it but chairs and a long table. "This is where the cowboys eat," Aunt Betty told him.

She showed him another room. It was small, and the walls were of pine. There was an Indian rug on the floor. By the side of the bed was a table. Under the table was a chest covered with leather. When Danny went to the window to look out, he could see the flat-topped mountain.

"I like this room best of all," he said.

39

"I am glad you do," said Aunt Betty. "This is your room."

Uncle Mack came in. "Have you looked in the chest?" he asked. "There is something in it for you."

Danny got down on his knees and opened the chest.

"Oh!" he said. "Here's a hat."

It was a cowboy hat. He put it on.

"See what else is in the chest," said Uncle Mack.

Danny took out a red handkerchief.

"To wear around your neck," said Aunt Betty.

He took out a blue-and-white checked shirt and a pair of blue jeans. Next he took out a pair of leather chaps. In the bottom of the chest he found a pair of fine, new cowboy boots!

Uncle Mack helped him put on his new clothes. He showed him how to put the chaps on over his jeans.

"A cowboy doesn't wear these clothes just to dress up," said Uncle Mack. "He wears a wide hat to keep off the sun and rain. He wears a handkerchief around his neck to keep out the dust."

"What are chaps for?" asked Danny.

"Sometimes a cowboy has to ride through brush,"

40

said Uncle Mack. "When he wears chaps, the thorns can't stick him and brush can't hit him on the legs."

Danny looked at his boots. "Why does a cowboy wear boots with high heels?"

"So his feet will fit better in the stirrups when he rides," said Uncle Mack. "I'll show you about that tomorrow."

Danny walked around in his new clothes. "Now I'm a cowboy!"

Uncle Mack laughed. "It takes more than clothes to make a cowboy."

"Will you show me how to be a cowboy?" asked Danny.

41

"Yes," said Uncle Mack. "We'll start tomorrow. Why don't you sit down now and write a letter home?" So Danny got out paper and pencil. He sat down at the table and wrote:

Dear Mother and Father:

I am at the ranch. I like it here. Uncle Mack and Aunt Betty gave me cowboy clothes, but I am not a cowboy yet. I am going to start tomorrow.

Your son,

Danny

WHAT HAPPENED?

Father and Mother had a big surprise for Danny. He couldn't guess what it was. When Uncle Mack came, he soon found out. What was the big surprise? Did you guess it before Danny?

Uncle Mack told Danny about the clothes that cowboys wear. Everything a cowboy wears helps him in his work. How do the cowboy's clothes help him?

THINK IT OVER

Not everybody can be a cowboy. Not everybody wants to be. What do you want to be when you grow up? Do you know much about it? Could your father or mother tell you about it?

42

WHAT DOES A COWBOY DO?

CLYDE BULLA

What does a cow-boy do all day?
What does a cow-boy do at night?

What does a cow-boy do all day?
What does a cow-boy do at night?

Rides in the pas-ture far a way With the
Sleeps and dreams till broad day-light Of the

cat-tle on the range. Yip-pee i-
cat-tle on the range. Yip-pee i-

ay! Yip-pee - i - ay!
ay! Yip-pee - i - ay!

From *Surprise for a Cowboy* by Clyde Robert Bulla. Copyright, 1950, by Clyde Robert Bulla. Reprinted by permission of the publisher, Thomas Y. Crowell Company.

43

BREAD AND MOLASSES

Carolyn Haywood

On Saturday mornings Betsy played with her little friends. Sometimes she went to Ellen's house and sometimes to Billy Porter's. Sometimes Ellen or Billy came to play at Betsy's.

Billy had a new puppy-dog. The dog had been named Miss Mopsie-Upsie Tail because her tail stuck up so straight. Most of the time she was called Mopsie for short because nobody could go out front and call, "Here, Miss Mopsie-Upsie Tail! Here, Miss Mopsie-Upsie Tail!" Billy had a lot of different ways of calling her. Sometimes he shouted, "Here, Mopsie-Upsie-Opsie," and sometimes he would call, "Here, Upsie-Opsie-Mopsie" and sometimes, "Here, Opsie-Mopsie-Upsie," so

that Miss Mopsie-Upsie Tail soon learned to run home whenever she heard anything shouted with a lot of p's in it.

One Saturday morning Mother drove into the city. She dropped Betsy off at Billy's house. Billy's mother had invited Betsy to spend the whole day with Billy. Betsy had her paintbox with her, for she and Billy had decided to color pictures in a new painting book. They both liked to paint, and whenever they painted pictures that pleased them very much they would climb up three flights of stairs to the top floor of Billy's house to show their work to Billy's father. Billy's father was an artist and he worked all day painting pictures in his studio away up on the top floor.

About ten o'clock Billy's mother looked into the living room. The two children were lying on the floor painting. Mopsie was lying as close to the children as she could. She was almost on top of the painting book.

"I am going to the store now," said Billy's mother. "Don't disturb Daddy because he is very busy this morning."

"Can we have something to eat?" asked Billy.

"Yes," replied his mother. "I left some crackers for you on the kitchen table."

Mrs. Porter went off and the two children ran out to the kitchen. They finished off the crackers in no time.

"Say!" said Billy. "We have some dandy molasses. Do you like bread and molasses, Betsy?"

"You bet!" said Betsy.

"Well, I'll see if I can find it," said Billy.

Billy looked in the refrigerator but the molasses was not there. Finally, up on a high shelf, he spied a jar filled with golden molasses. Billy climbed up on a chair and reached for the jar. He couldn't quite reach it. Betsy and Mopsie stood by, looking up at Billy. Billy stood on his toes and stretched as high as he could. Now he could

touch the jar. He moved it with his fingers to the edge of the shelf. Now he could get his hand around it. Very carefully he lifted the jar down.

"Oh, boy!" said Billy, as he placed the jar on the table, "I was afraid I was going to drop it."

"I was holding my breath," said Betsy.

Billy took the lid off the jar. "Now we'll get some bread," said Billy, opening the breadbox.

Mopsie had her two front paws against the edge of the table. She didn't want to miss anything, especially not anything to eat.

"Here's the bread," said Billy, handing the loaf to Betsy.

As Betsy reached for the loaf of bread, her elbow knocked against the jar of molasses. Over it went, pouring the golden syrup over the edge of the table right on top of Mopsie. In a moment the molasses was all over Mopsie's back.

"Now look what you did," shouted Billy. "What will my mother say?"

Betsy stood the jar up and looked at the sticky mess. Then she looked at Mopsie. The molasses that had fallen on Mopsie's head was now running down over her face. The rest was settling into Mopsie's fur coat.

"Have you got a rag?" asked Betsy. "I'll wipe it up."

Billy gave Betsy the dishcloth and Betsy wiped the molasses off the table. Then she wiped up all that had gotten on the floor.

"Now you will have to wipe Mopsie," said Billy.

Betsy reached for the little dog, but Mopsie thought Betsy wanted to play so she turned and ran. Through the kitchen door she flew. Round and round the dining-room table she dashed. The children ran after her shouting, "Here, Mopsie! Come here!"

Mopsie was having a good time. This was more fun than watching the children color picture books. She flew out into the hall and up the stairs. The children raced after her. Mopsie dashed into Mrs. Porter's bedroom and jumped right into the center of the bed. To Betsy's horror, Mopsie rolled all over the clean white bedspread. Before Billy could pick the little dog up, the bedspread was

ruined. There were sticky yellow spots all over it.

Billy clutched Mopsie tightly in his arms. "We'll have to give her a bath," said Billy. "She's sticky all over."

Billy carried the dog into the bathroom. "Turn on the water," he said.

Betsy put the stopper in the tub and turned on the water. She let it run until the tub was half full. Then Billy put Mopsie into the water and the two children set to work. Betsy held Mopsie while

Billy washed her. He rubbed soapflakes all over Mopsie until she was covered with lather. Then he rinsed the soapsuds off with clear water. As he lifted the dog out of the tub, Billy knocked against the towel rack. Down went the guest towels into the water.

"Gee!" said Billy, "now look what I did!"

Billy set Mopsie down on the floor and leaned over to pick up the wet towels. Like a flash, Mopsie was off again. Back to the bedroom she scampered leaving wet tracks behind her. The children ran shrieking after her, but before they could catch her she was up on Mrs. Porter's bed again, rolling on the molasses-spotted bedspread. Billy caught her and carried her back to the bathroom. Once again he put Mopsie in the tub and rinsed her off. "Now you hold her," he said to Betsy when he lifted Mopsie out.

Betsy held her while Billy rubbed Mopsie with his own towel. Then he carried her down to the kitchen and put her in her bed. "Now you stay there," he said, "and behave yourself."

51

When Billy came upstairs again, Betsy said, "What will your mother say about the bedspread?"

Billy looked at the bedspread. It was certainly a sorry sight. "Maybe we better wash it," said Billy.

"Maybe we better," said Betsy.

The children took the bedspread off the bed and carried it into the bathroom. They put it in the tub and added more soapflakes. They both rubbed it as hard as they could. When they thought that it was clean, they tried to lift it out of the water but the water made it so heavy they couldn't lift the bedspread.

By this time Billy and Betsy were soaking wet. Betsy's dress was sticking to her and water was dropping off the bottom of Billy's shorts. Betsy's braids had gone into the water so many times that her whole head felt wet. Once more they tried to lift the spread but it was no use. They were not strong enough.

"Perhaps we could lift it if we got into the tub," said Betsy.

"All right," said Billy.

The children took off their shoes and stockings and stepped into the tub. Again they tried to lift the heavy spread. They found that they could each lift one end, but no matter how hard they

pulled, they couldn't lift the spread out of the tub.

"Now heave," shouted Billy. Betsy heaved. Billy heaved so hard that he sat down in the tub. This upset Betsy and she went down with a splash.

"Daddy!" cried Billy, at the top of his voice. "Daddy, Daddy, Daddy!"

Mr. Porter came down the stairs three steps at a time. When he reached the bathroom door, the two children were standing up in the tub. They looked like drowned rats.

"What's going on?" said Mr. Porter.

"Come help us, Daddy," said Billy. "Come help us."

Mr. Porter squeezed the water out of the children's clothes. Then he helped them out of the tub. Meanwhile Billy and Betsy told him what had happened.

"Betsy, you will have to take off your clothes and put on some of Billy's dry clothes," said Mr. Porter.

Billy trotted off to his room to change his clothes and his father got some clothes for Betsy to put on. While the children were dressing, he wrung the water out of the bedspread, the guest towels, and the children's clothes. Then he washed out Billy's towel that Billy had used to dry Mopsie.

53

When Billy's mother came home, Mr. Porter was hanging Billy's towel on the clothesline.

Mrs. Porter looked at the clothesline. She opened her mouth in surprise. There were the bedspread, the guest towels, all of Billy's clothes, and all of Betsy's clothes. In the doorway stood Billy and Betsy dressed like little brothers.

"What happened?" said Billy's mother.

"I just wanted to give Betsy a piece of bread and molasses," said Billy.

"Well, everything is on the line but the dog," said Billy's daddy.

WHAT HAPPENED?

Billy and Betsy really had a sticky time. They didn't have molasses on bread. They had molasses on Mopsie. What did they do?

Finally Mopsie was clean. Did she stay out of trouble? Who finally came to help?

THINK IT OVER

Billy and Betsy were left to take care of themselves. Daddy was busy upstairs. He didn't know what they were doing. Do you think Billy and Betsy should have called Father when trouble first started? Why? What do you do when you spill something?

THE HUT

Hilda Van Stockum

We built a hut, my brother and I,
Over a sandy pit,
With twigs that bowed and met above
And leaves to cover it.

And there we sat when all around
The rain came pouring down.
We knew if we were out in it
We'd both be sure to drown.

And though in puddles at our feet
Drops gathered from the sky,
We smiled through strands of dripping hair,
Because we felt so dry.

Reprinted by permission of *The Horn Book Magazine*.

THE MOON

May Morgan

I like to sit on our doorsill,
And watch the place above the hill
Get lighter every minute till
The moon comes up all bright and still.

Sometimes he is so slow, I think
He'll never come: then, in a wink,
Almost behind the big oak tree,
He pops right up, and smiles at me.

UNIT TWO

ANIMAL FRIENDS

FOUND,

THE LITTLE LOST DOG

Val Teal

Mother took John and Peter downtown to buy new shoes. They parked their car and got out. A little gray dog was sitting on the sidewalk. He sniffed at John and Peter and whined. They patted his head. He jumped up and tried to lick their faces.

"He likes us," Peter said. "Can't we keep him for our dog?"

"No," Mother said. "He's lost. The people who lost him will be looking for him."

When they came back from buying the shoes, the little gray dog was still there. They patted his head.

"Poor little lost dog," they said.

The little lost dog wagged his tail.

"Can't we keep him for our dog?" John said.

"No," Mother said. "He isn't our dog."

From *Read Me More Stories*, compiled by the Child Study Association of America. Copyright, 1951, by Thomas Y. Crowell Company, publishers.

59

Mother opened the car door. John got in. Peter got in. Mother got in. And then, when nobody was looking, the little lost dog got in. He snuggled down on the floor in the back seat.

When they got home Mother got out of the car. John got out. Peter got out. He left the car door open. The little lost dog got out.

"Look!" Peter said. "It's the little lost dog! He followed us home."

The little gray dog shivered.

"Can't he come in and get warm?" John asked.

"Yes," Mother said. "Poor little lost dog."

They found an old rug and put it in the back hall. The little lost dog lay down on it. They found an old blanket and covered him up. The little lost dog went to sleep.

"We found a little lost dog," Peter said.

"He needs a bath," Father said.

They gave the little gray dog a bath. They washed him with soap. They rubbed him with a towel. He stood on the floor and shook himself.

He wasn't a little gray dog! He was a little white dog! With pink linings in his ears. And a little black nose with pink edges. And a long pink tongue. And beautiful big brown eyes.

They fed him and gave him a saucer of milk.

"Can't we keep him?" Peter asked.

"He isn't our dog," Father said. "We must try
to find his owners."

They looked in the evening paper. Nobody
had advertised for a little lost white dog.

"Can we keep him now?" John asked.

"No," Father said. "We must try to find his
owners."

They took him to a place where all the lost
dogs are. They left him there to see if his
owners would come and get him. They left him
there three days.

61

After three days they went back. There was the little lost dog. Nobody had come to get him. He was sitting in the corner of a pen. He looked very lost. He looked very sad.

When he saw them, he jumped up and ran to meet them. He licked their hands.

"Poor little lost dog," Peter said.

"He isn't lost any more," Father said.

"Can we keep him?" John and Peter shouted.

"Yes," Father said. "Now he is our dog."

They took the little lost dog home. He snuggled down on the rug in the back hall. They covered him up with the blanket. He went to sleep. He looked very happy. He didn't look lost.

"Look," Peter said. "He's found."

So they named the little lost dog Found. And, to this very day, Found is living with John and Peter and sleeping on the rug in the back hall.

THINK IT OVER

John and Peter found a little lost puppy. They took good care of him. How do you take care of your dog or pet? John and Peter gave a funny name to their dog. What is your pet's name? How did you choose the name you gave to your pet?

BABY BEARS

E. Charushin

In the middle of a great forest in northern Russia is the small village of Little Pines.

One winter day some hunters from Little Pines came upon a bear's den in the forest. There was a huge old bear in the den. Of course the hunters shot her. Then they packed up the fur and the meat to take home with them.

But when the hunters were ready to leave, they noticed two small furry lumps in the corner of the den. They were two baby bears, as big as your hand.

One of the men picked up the two little bears in his hands. He said, "I'll take them home to my wife. Won't she be surprised!"

Then he put both of the bears in his cap and carried them home that way.

From *Baby Bears* by E. Charushin, translated from the Russian by Marguerita Rudolph. Reprinted by permission of The Macmillan Company, publishers.

When the man walked into his cottage with a hatful of bears, his wife, Ivanovna, clapped her hands in great surprise. The man laughed. He emptied the cap with the bears onto an old sheepskin coat under the bench.

And there the baby bears lived.

Ivanovna filled some bottles with warm milk and corked them up with pieces of soft old cloth. The little bears lay on the warm sheepskin and held the bottles in their mouths. They sucked the milk through the soft cloth all day long, making loud smacking sounds. When tired they closed their baby eyes and slept a little. Then they sucked again.

For a few weeks the baby bears didn't move away from the sheepskin at all. Then they rolled a little and took a few steps. Soon they started crawling and waddling, going a little farther each day.

"The little bears are getting along very well!" said Ivanovna one day. . . .

By summer they were bigger than cats. Then

64

they grew to be the size of small dogs. As they grew bigger they got into more and more mischief.

One of them would tip a soup pot on the table. The pot would roll and crack so that the hot cabbage soup would spill on Ivanovna or her husband. The other bear would hide the iron pot fork. Ivanovna wouldn't miss it until the minute she was in a hurry to push a pot into the hot brick oven. Then she would have to crawl under the bed to find it!

Both of the bears loved to pull feathers out of Ivanovna's best pillows. Just think of what a mess that made! They gave the poor woman no rest. When they were not up to mischief they were tumbling and rolling on the floor under her feet.

At last Ivanovna chased them out of the cottage.

"Run along," she said. "Have all your fun outdoors! If the dogs chase you — you can fight them off with your strong paws, or climb up somewhere where the dogs can't reach you. Off with you now!"

So the two small bears started living a free life in the village streets. You would think they would try running into the forest. But they never did. Ivanovna's cottage was their den, their home. If they were caught in some trouble outdoors, or someone frightened them, the bears instantly ran into the cottage and crawled under the bench on their own sheepskin. . . .

"Oh me!" cried Ivanovna. "I wish there was a way of selling the naughty bears to the city."

Well, going to the city from Little Pines is easier said than done. In the spring the snow melts. Then the roads are just thick muddy rivers. In the summer there is too much work to do. No one would be riding to the city then. And in

the winter the high snowbanks and the hungry animals make a trip to the city unsafe. So the bears had to stay on in the village.

One day that summer, however, a hunter happened to come along to Little Pines. The first story he heard people tell was about Ivanovna's tame bears. The hunter went straight to Ivanovna's cottage. He expected her to show him the bears. But, instead, she told him in a tired voice to look for the bears outside somewhere.

The hunter walked all through the streets looking for the bears. He couldn't find them anywhere.

"Well," he thought, "they must have run away into the forest. They probably aren't really tame."

67

At that moment — bang! A heavy brick fell under the hunter's nose. He quickly jumped aside and looked up at the nearby roof.

There, in the middle, sat two small brown bears. They were very busy taking the chimney apart, brick by brick. They took turns pulling bricks out and letting them slide off the roof. They even put their heads down to listen to the scraping sliding noise that the bricks made. One of the bears stuck his tongue out. He almost laughed with pleasure at the sound.

Seeing the mischief, the hunter quickly ran into the cottage to tell Ivanovna. . . .

That evening three angry neighbors came. The bears had taken their chimneys apart and pushed the bricks down. Then when the fires were made all the smoke came back into the cottages instead of going outside.

At last poor Ivanovna started crying. She sobbed, and wiped her eyes and nose with her embroidered linen apron.

"See for yourself," she said to the hunter, "what mischief they are apt to do. When they were little they were harmless babies. Now I can't put

up with them. Please, sir, take them away with you," she begged.

The hunter agreed. Tying ropes around the bears' necks, he led them out of the village. When they came near the forest, the hunter decided to untie the ropes so that the bears would be free to run off into the forest.

But what do you think happened?

The bears were afraid of the strange forest! They sniffed and turned away from it. They rubbed and pushed against the man. They wouldn't move away from him.

The hunter saw that the bears wouldn't leave him, so he took them to the city. They walked along for two whole days, staying close to the man. When they came to the city, the hunter put a rope around the bears and led them again.

Before long, dogs ran out from every street corner barking and following the bears. Soon the children heard the noise and ran out from everywhere. They stared and shouted and pointed their fingers at the bears. Grownups, too, stopped to watch. In fact, the whole city turned out in a parade.

At last the hunter came to the zoo and sold the bears. He got a hundred rubles for the pair!

The zoo-keeper was kind to the baby bears. . . . And they lived in the zoo happily a long while.

WHAT HAPPENED?

One of the hunters took the baby bears home to his wife, Ivanovna. How did Ivanovna take care of the baby bears when they were little?

The bears grew older. They became full of mischief. What did they do to tease Ivanovna?

At last a hunter came to town. He wanted to see the bears. Where did he find them? What were they doing? The hunter said he would take the bears to the city. What did he do with them there? Were the bears happy?

THINK IT OVER

Everybody likes to make a fuss over a baby. When babies grow a little older, they sometimes get into mischief. Perhaps you have a little brother or sister. Can you remember something he did to tease you? A baby must learn how to grow up into a good boy or girl. How can you help the baby grow up into a good boy or girl?

FAMILIAR FRIENDS

James S. Tippett

The horses, the pigs,
And the chickens,
The turkeys, the ducks,
And the sheep!
I can see all my friends
From my window
As soon as I waken
From sleep.

The cat on the fence
Is out walking.
The geese have gone down
For a swim.
The pony comes trotting
Right up to the gate;
He knows I have candy
For him.

The cows in the pasture
Are switching
Their tails to keep off
The flies.
And the old mother dog
Has come out in the yard
With five pups to give me a surprise.

From *I Spend the Summer* by James S. Tippett. Copyright, 1930, by Harper & Brothers.

LONESOME ROSIE

Lilian Moore and Leone Adelson

Rosie, the horse, was growing old. Farmer Dilly put her out to pasture and bought a truck to do her work. He hoped Rosie would have a good time.

"Yes," said Farmer Dilly. "Rosie has worked long and well. Now she's going to have a good time."

And Rosie did have a good time — for a few days. How nice it was to sleep late every morning! What fun it was to run and chase the rabbits! How good it was to roll in the cool grass and feel it on her hot back! She had nothing to do all day but to sleep, to run, to eat, and to play.

But every day she did the same things.

After a while it was not quite so much fun to have nothing more to do. Nothing to do but run after rabbits. Nothing to do but sleep in the barn or roll in the grass — all by herself.

One morning she stood and watched Farmer Dilly drive off in his new red truck. He had no time for Rosie now. No time to say, "Good morning, Rosie. How's my old girl today?" No time to pet her and give her something sweet to eat. Now it was the truck that went down the good hard road in the quiet morning. It was the truck that saw all the things and people on the way. But who would want to say "Good morning" to a truck? And how could a truck say anything to Prince as it went by the Winterberry farm? How could the friendly train men pet the new red truck?

Rosie missed all these things. She missed the run down the road to the milk train, and all the things and the people on the way. But most of all she missed Farmer Dilly.

Rosie did not know it, but she was lonesome.

Perhaps that is why she came to do the things she did.

It all began one day when Rosie thought she just *had* to see Farmer Dilly. She could not get out through the gate — the gate was closed. She

could not jump over the fence — the fence was too high. But away off in the field was an old stone wall that was falling down. Rosie looked at it for a long time. Yes, it would be easy to jump over that. She gave a little run and a jump. Over she went, and down the road to the farm house.

How happy she was! She was going to see the Dilly family. And how happy they would be to see her. They must miss her, too.

Oh dear, there was no one in the front yard. Maybe there was someone in the back yard. She looked — no one was there. Then Rosie saw that the cellar door was open. Perhaps she would find someone down there. She walked over and looked down the stairs. It was very quiet, but sniff! sniff! What was that wonderful smell? It was the most wonderful smell of all — the strong sweet smell of fresh apples.

Do you know how good a hot dog smells to a hungry boy? That is how apples smelled to Rosie. Before she knew it she was down the steps and in the cellar. And there they were — a pan full of big red apples!

74

How good they were! Every one of them — down to the very last one. Rosie stood there, full of apples, feeling good and a little sleepy. She heard some people walking around upstairs and talking. That was good, too. Her head dropped down, her eyes closed, and soon she was fast asleep.

Up in the kitchen Grandma Dilly was about to bake a pie.

"Ah!" said Mr. Dilly. "Pie for supper — I hope it's apple pie."

"That's just what it is going to be." Grandma laughed. "I have a nice pan of my best apples down in the cellar. I have been keeping them just for a pie," she said. "I'll go down and get them now."

75

Grandma was halfway down the cellar steps when Mr. and Mrs. Dilly heard her scream.

All Grandma saw in the cellar at first was a big dark Something. All Rosie knew was that a scream woke her out of a quiet nap. Before Grandma knew that the Something was only Rosie, she had run all the way back up to the kitchen. And before Rosie knew that it was only Grandma, she had been frightened out of the cellar and was running down the road back to the barn.

Farmer Dilly looked out the window just in time to see Rosie go down the road.

"There goes Rosie!" cried Farmer Dilly. "What has she been up to?"

As soon as they found the apples gone they understood what had happened.

"My, what a fright she gave me!" said Grandma Dilly again and again. "And eating all my best apples, too!"

"That's a funny thing for Rosie to do," said Farmer Dilly. "She never did anything like that before."

Mrs. Dilly was puzzled, too. "She gets plenty to eat. Why is she so greedy?" she said. "I guess we will just have to keep the cellar door closed."

Rosie had been so frightened that for a few days she stayed close to the barn. But soon she

76

began to feel lonesome and unhappy again.

No one came near her. She did not want to run or play or roll in the grass. She did not even want to chase the funny little rabbits that ran by. More than anything, she wanted to be with someone she loved. So one day Rosie jumped over the wall again and trotted down the road to the farm house.

There was a car in front of the house, but no people. Rosie trotted around to the back of the house. Nobody there! Nothing to do but wait. She looked around. There were some pretty flowers in the window box. M-m-m, they smelled good. M-m-m, they tasted good, too. She ate them all, and then put her head through the open window. Maybe there would be some more inside. Rosie looked around, and then she saw the Thing!

It was a pretty yellow Thing, and on it was a big red flower. How nice! More flowers! They were not good to eat, but the yellow Thing smelled just like hay. It tasted just like hay, too, so Rosie ate it all up. No — not quite all, for almost at the last bite, Mrs. Dilly walked into the room with her friend, Mrs. Winterberry.

How glad Rosie was to see someone at last! She put her head as far into the room as she could, hoping Mrs. Dilly would pet her and say, "Hello,

Rosie." But all at once there was a loud cry from Mrs. Winterberry.

"Oh, look — my hat — she's eating my new hat! Get my hat!"

Poor Rosie! They rushed at her so fast that she was frightened. She pulled her head out of the window, turned, and ran down the road, jumped over the wall, and went right into the barn.

When Farmer Dilly got home that night, what a story he heard! Mrs. Dilly was quite upset.

"It was Mrs. Winterberry's very best hat," she told him. "The one with the big red flower!"

Farmer Dilly tried not to laugh, but he could not help it. He laughed and laughed.

"It's not funny," said Mrs. Dilly. "Mrs. Winterberry is very angry."

"Well," said Farmer Dilly, still laughing, "I always thought that was a mighty funny hat."

"Maybe so," said Grandma, "but I'd like to know — what *is* the matter with that horse? Coming right to the house! Eating my best apples! Eating Mrs. Winterberry's best hat!"

"I told you she was a greedy old horse," said Mrs. Dilly, still upset about the hat.

"Yes, sir, that was some hat!" said Farmer Dilly, and he laughed again. . . .

Rosie did not know what was going to happen

the next day but she was very unhappy. Why couldn't she and Farmer Dilly have good times together any more? Why did something always go wrong? All she wanted was to be near the family. But every time she went to see them someone got angry at her. Someone always shouted at her. Nobody petted her any more. It almost seemed that no one loved her any more.

Rosie walked out of the barn and looked over the fence at the house. It was a beautiful night. The stars were out and the moon was bright. The old horse could not sleep. All she could think of was Farmer Dilly's angry face. She had a feeling that she must go back to the house. They must not be so angry at her.

Once more she jumped over the wall and walked slowly and sadly to the house. The house was dark and very quiet. Everyone was asleep. Everything was closed tight to keep her out. How lonely she was!

But there! One window was open in the back of the house. And something was moving in the window. Maybe someone was up, after all. Could it be Grandma? No — too big. Could it be Mrs. Dilly? No, it was a man. Oh, it must be Farmer Dilly! But no, this was a fat man. Rosie did not know who it was, but she was glad to see someone at last. Maybe the man had an apple for her. Maybe he would even pet her!

Rosie walked up to the window. It was not a very big window and the man was getting out a little at a time. First came a leg. Then his shoulder. Rosie came closer to look. When the man turned to jump, he found himself looking right into Rosie's big brown eyes. He was so surprised that he let go, and fell right back into the room! "Now where is he?" thought Rosie. She put her head through the open window. There he was, sitting on the kitchen floor.

Rosie made a friendly noise.

"Sh! Nice horsey!" the man whispered. "Go back to your barn like a good horse."

Rosie nodded her head to show the man that she was glad he liked her and to tell him she liked him, too.

"No, no! Go away!" the man whispered again. "Go away like a good girl."

Rosie tried to get closer to this nice man.

"Get away from that window, you stupid horse!" the man said, getting angry. "I've got to get out of here!"

But Rosie just stood at the window, trying to make friends.

Suddenly the man saw the other kitchen window. He ran to open it.

"This is a good game!" thought Rosie. So she trotted around the house to the other window, too. The man was almost out of the window when Rosie got there. She pulled at his leg playfully as if to say, "Here I am!"

"Ouch! Let go of my leg!" the man cried out. "Let go or I'll fall!"

81

And he did! Right out of the window and right on top of Grandma Dilly's flower pots. CRASH! BANG! went the man. SMASH! BANG! went the flower pots!

Suddenly three windows opened upstairs.

"Who's there?" called Farmer Dilly.

"What is it?" called Mrs. Dilly.

"What's going on down there?" called Grandma Dilly.

Rosie looked up. There was her family! She was so glad to see them that she forgot all about the man.

"Who's that down there?" called Farmer Dilly.

"There's a man running away!" screamed Mrs. Dilly.

"Catch him! Catch him!" cried Grandma.

But by the time they all got downstairs and turned on the lights, the man had run down the road and was out of sight.

"Look!" said Grandma Dilly. "The kitchen windows are open!"

"Our house has been robbed!" cried Mrs. Dilly. "Oh! Oh! My clock! My good spoons! Where are they?"

"Maybe they are in here," said Farmer Dilly, picking up a brown bag from the floor. "It looks as if the robber had to go in a hurry. He didn't have time to take this with him." He opened the bag and there were the spoons and the clock. And then he held up an old tin box. "Am I glad to see this!" he said.

"Why should anyone want to take that old thing?" asked Mrs. Dilly.

Farmer Dilly opened the box. "Because it has all this money in it! I was going to take it to the bank in the morning. It's a good thing that robber was frightened away!"

"What ever do you suppose frightened him?" Grandma wanted to know.

"It must have been Rosie!" said Mrs. Dilly. "When we looked out, she was standing by the window."

"Good old Rosie!" said Farmer Dilly. "Where is she now?"

Rosie was back in the barn. She had seen the family come out to the yard. But they had not talked to her. No one seemed to care about her. So she had gone sadly away.

And then suddenly the barn door opened. There they stood — Farmer Dilly, Mrs. Dilly, and Grandma Dilly, smiling at her. In Farmer Dilly's hand there were two big red apples.

"Here, old Rosie," he said in his old friendly way. "If not for you, our house would have been robbed of many things tonight. Thank you, old girl."

Rosie put out her head and sniffed at the apples, but she did not eat them. She took a few steps until she was close to Farmer Dilly. Then she put

her old head down on his shoulder. Rosie was happy again.

"Why look!" said Mrs. Dilly. "Rosie's not eating the apples. That's funny!"

Grandma Dilly shook her head. "No," she said. "It's not funny at all. I think I know why Rosie has been doing such silly things. She didn't come for apples, or for Mrs. Winterberry's hat. She isn't greedy. She's just lonely, that's all. That's why she came to the house again and again."

"And each time we frightened her away," said Mrs. Dilly sadly.

"That was no way to treat an old friend, was it, Rosie?" said Farmer Dilly. "It wasn't very kind to leave you all alone, was it?" He patted her head. "I know what we can do," he said. "We'll put you in that field right next to the house.

85

Then we can talk to you whenever we pass by, and you can watch us coming and going."

"Why yes!" cried Mrs. Dilly. "And at night we can take you back to the barn to sleep where it's warm. How's that, Rosie dear?"

But Rosie did not hear Mrs. Dilly. She was eating the big red apples now. She had her family around her, and they loved her again.

That was enough for old Rosie!

WHAT HAPPENED?

Rosie liked people. She wanted to be near them.

At first Mr. and Mrs. Dilly and Grandma didn't understand. Rosie tried to get attention with the apples and Mrs. Winterberry's hat. What did she do to the apples and Mrs. Winterberry's hat?

Still Mr. and Mrs. Dilly and Grandma didn't understand. It took a burglar to help them understand what Rosie really wanted. How did the burglar do that? Then what did Farmer Dilly do for Rosie?

THINK IT OVER

You don't have to be old to be lonesome. Sometimes you are lonesome, too. Rosie wanted to be near friends when she was lonesome. What helps you when you feel lonesome?

86

MY DOG

Tom Robinson

My dog listens when I talk.
He goes with me for a walk.
When I sleep, he's sleepy too.
He does everything I do.
He has eyes that always show
He knows everything I know.
I never do a thing but he
Thinks it is all right for me.
When I speak, he always minds.
He shares with me the things he finds.
When other people say I'm bad,
He hangs his head and looks so sad.
He cuddles up and laps my hand
And tells me he can understand.

HAMLET'S EARS

Irma Simonton Black

Once there was a dog named Hamlet. He was
a very black dog, a very small black dog. When
you looked at Hamlet you noticed his ears.
Hamlet's ears were the largest part of him. They
were long ears, softer and silkier than a little girl's
hair.

People used to look at Hamlet and say, "What
long and lovely ears he has!"

But day by day Hamlet grew sadder and sadder.
He had a rather long face anyhow, but when
Hamlet thought about his ears, his face grew so
sad that you expected him to cry. Then his ears
drooped until they hung longer than ever.

Sometimes Hamlet would sigh softly to himself
as he lay on the rug by the radiator, his nose on

From *Hamlet, A Cocker Spaniel*, by Irma Simonton Black. Reprinted by permission of
Holiday House, publishers.

his front paws, and his ears (of course) trailing on the floor.

Sometimes Hamlet would sigh softly and whisper (though no one ever heard him),

> "I've grown quite thin.
> And I'll grow thinner
> Because my ears
> Drag in my dinner."

That, you see, was the sort of ears Hamlet had. You wouldn't like to have your ears trail in your dinner, would you? But Hamlet couldn't help himself. He couldn't even hold his ears back when he ate his dinner. He couldn't pin them back, as ladies do their hair, and he couldn't tie them back, as little girls do their hair.

Hamlet's ears sometimes had gravy on them when he finished eating. Sometimes they had milk. If he drank water the black hair on his ears grew very wet. Then before he fell asleep after dinner, he would sigh and whisper, his eyes half-shut,

> "I'm getting lean.
> And I'll grow leaner
> Because my ears
> Will not stay cleaner."

This was the sad story of Hamlet all through the first year he was alive.

Then one day in the summer it was very, very hot. It was so hot that Hamlet did not chase flies nor ask to go out. He lay inside on the cool bricks in front of the fireplace. He lay very still but his sides moved when he breathed and his pink tongue hung out over two sharp teeth. He felt too warm even to whisper about his ears, which by this time had grown longer than before.

While Hamlet was lying there, he heard footsteps coming in from the hall. Wag-wag went his tail. His ears told him whose footsteps they were. The black tip of his nose twitched a very little.

Wag-wag went his tail again, for it was his master. Usually Hamlet jumped up when his master came in, but this time he was so hot that he lay with just his tail moving.

90

Hamlet's master was saying, "You're too hot, old fellow. Come outside and we'll take some of your fur coat off."

Hamlet's master took big scissors like the ones the barber cuts your hair with. They went out on the grass. Hamlet's master cut off the feathery hair along Hamlet's legs and the thick curls off his back. Hamlet could feel a little breeze on his body. Then Hamlet's master looked at his ears.

You see, he thought Hamlet's ears were very beautiful. He did not like to cut off any of the long hair that grew on them.

Then he clipped some hair off each ear to make Hamlet cooler. Hamlet stood very still until the hair came off his ears. Then he knew that they felt lighter.

91

He shook his head hard, he ran up and down the yard.

As he ran by, he barked to his master,

"Perhaps I'm loud
Perhaps I'm rollicking
But short ears make
Me feel like frolicking!"

That night, Hamlet ate dinner. His ears did not (quite) reach his plate.

WHAT HAPPENED?

Sometimes Hamlet was sad. Why was he unhappy part of the time? One hot day his master did something to help Hamlet. Tell what his master did.

THINK IT OVER

Hamlet made up poems about his ears. It is really easy to make a poem. Below is the first line of a poem. What words can you think of that would rhyme with *sad*? Try to make up a second line to make a poem. Do *not* write in your book.

"Hamlet, the dog, was sometimes sad,

_____."

BUZZIE GOES
TO HIS NEW HOME

Ann Petry

Buzzie was a round, fat kitten. His fur was gray with touches of yellow under his chin and on his paws. He was just the color of smoke as it comes up from a pile of burning leaves.

He had a very short tail and a very loud purr. When he was happy he purred so loudly that he sounded exactly like a small warm motor — buzz-zz, buzz-zz, buzz-zz. That is why he was called Buzzie.

His first home was in a big red barn. He lived there with his mother and his three brothers and two sisters.

One morning his mother washed him all over, very carefully, while she told him that he was going to have a new home; and that he was to go to his new home that night.

"It's in a drugstore, Buzzie," his mother said. "And you must mind your manners so that Miss James and her brother, Mr. James, will like you. It's a very good place to live."

Buzzie got so excited at the thought of going somewhere brand new that he skipped away from his mother before she finished washing his face. He ran over to his brothers and sisters to tell them that he was going away.

"I never did think much of this as a place to live," Buzzie said, staring at the wisps of hay on the barn floor. "I'm going to live in a drugstore. I bet you wish *you* were," he said to the other kittens.

He could tell by the way they tumbled against him, and by the questions they asked, that they wanted to go away with him. He never once thought that he might miss his mother and these brothers and sisters after he reached his new home. But he did wonder how he would get back to the barn if he decided he didn't want to stay at the drugstore.

So he ran back to his mother. "What will I do if I don't like living in a drugstore?" he asked.

His mother half closed her eyes and looked very wise. She began washing his right ear. He tried to wriggle away from her. But she held him firmly with one paw.

"Oh, you'll like the drugstore," she said. "Of course you won't have anyone to talk to," her tongue moved down the side of his face. "But you'll get used to that."

"Why won't I have anyone to talk to?" Buzzie asked, alarmed. He drew closer to his mother although her tongue was very rough. She washed

95

a little harder around his right ear and he drew back.

"Because, my dear, human beings can't understand what cats say. You will be able to understand what they say. But they won't understand you."

"That's very queer," Buzzie said. "How will the people I'm going to live with know my name if they can't understand what I say?" he asked anxiously.

"Anyone who hears you purr will know that your name should be 'Buzzie.' And Miss James and her brother, Mr. James, who own the drugstore, are very bright people. They'll know your name once you purr very loudly for them."

"Why don't humans understand what cats say?" Buzzie asked.

"They just don't," his mother said flatly and changed the subject. "Now you remember that your father was a Manx cat —"

"What's a Manx cat?" Buzzie said, not waiting for her to finish what she was saying.

His mother sighed and gave him a gentle push, to remind him that he wasn't minding his manners.

"A Manx cat," she said, "is a cat with a short tail like yours. You look very much like your

father. He was a fine cat. And I expect you to make him proud of you."

Buzzie tried to peer around at his tail while his mother washed his neck. It was hard to do but he finally caught a glimpse of his tail. Then he looked at his brothers and sisters. Their tails were long. His tail was really very short.

He looked at his mother's tail. It was long and slender. As he looked at it she moved it gracefully.

"I want a long tail, too," he wailed.

"That's a very smart length tail you have," his mother said firmly. "There are very few cats with elegant short tails like that. Now you go to sleep so you'll be rested when Mr. James comes for you."

When Mr. James came to get Buzzie, it was dark outside. Buzzie's mother and his brothers and sisters stood in the barn door, watching, as Mr. James carried Buzzie out to his car.

The last thing Buzzie heard his mother say was, "Now remember! I've never had a kitten sent back to me. So you mind your manners!"

In the car, Buzzie purred very softly to show Mr. James that he wanted to be friendly. Then he said, "My name is Buzzie."

Mr. James did not answer. Buzzie stopped

97

purring and sat up straight in Mr. James's lap. "I wish I had someone to talk to," he said to himself.

The swaying motion of the car made him dizzy. The smell of gasoline got in his nose and he sneezed. It seemed to Buzzie that they rode for miles and miles, though they really didn't.

Finally the car stopped in front of the drugstore. The drugstore was in a building that was painted red. Lights shone out through the big glass window. Though Buzzie couldn't read it there was a big sign across the front of the building that said "James Drugstore" in shiny letters.

Mr. James carried Buzzie up the store steps so fast that Buzzie did not see the tall elm trees that lined the street, or a church across the way, with a white steeple that went up and up.

Mr. James walked straight through the drugstore, carrying Buzzie. When he reached a little room in the back, he put the kitten on the floor.

There were rows and rows of bottles on the shelves. At one end of the little room there was a long high counter with a stool in front of it.

Buzzie walked all around the little room, sniffing at the bottles on the floor. Then a woman with

99

gray hair came out of the drugstore and stood looking down at Buzzie over the top of her glasses. This was Miss James, Mr. James's sister.

"I wonder if *she* can understand me when I talk," Buzzie said under his breath. Then in his very best speaking voice he said, "I guess you must be Miss James. I'm your new cat." He looked up at her hopefully.

Miss James did not answer. Buzzie knew then that his mother had been right. Neither Mr. James nor Miss James could understand a word he said.

Miss James looked at her brother and said, "Why, that little cat has hardly any tail!"

Buzzie looked around at his short tail. It was really very short. His mother's tail was a beautiful length. But his mother had told him that this was a very smart length tail that he had.

He held his short tail straight up in order to make it look longer. Then he started walking in and out, in and out, between Mr. James's long legs.

"I don't think I'm going to like living in a drugstore," he said out loud, to himself. After all he had to have someone to talk to. "Miss James doesn't like my tail. And I haven't anyone to talk to."

He began thinking about the barn. His brothers and sisters would be lying in the sweet-smelling hay, curled up next to their mother. And right now she would be telling them stories, and purring songs to them. Oh, how he wished he was with them!

"Meow," he said, very sadly.

Miss James looked down at him over the top of her glasses. "He's got a very big voice for such a little cat," she said. Her eyebrows went up very high.

Someone came in the drugstore and Miss James went out of the little back room.

"I'm going to bed," Mr. James said. He leaned over and rubbed the top of Buzzie's small head. Then Mr. James went out of the little room, too.

Buzzie followed right behind Mr. James. They went up a long flight of stairs. When they reached the second floor, Buzzie walked away from Mr. James. He peered in the bedroom, stuck his paw inside a closet door, and then wandered out into a hall. He found another flight of stairs and went down them.

There was a dining room and a kitchen downstairs. He paused in front of the ice box in the kitchen and sniffed.

"I bet there's meat in there," he said to himself.

He poked his head through the living room door. The chairs looked soft, as though they might be good places to take a nap in.

"It's a little lonely over here," he said. "Guess I'll go back to the drugstore side."

He went up the stairs, through the hall, and came down the stairs on the other side of the building. Miss James was sitting in a chair by the window in the little back room.

Buzzie walked over to where she was sitting and looked up at her. "I suppose I have to try to make her want to keep me in spite of my short tail. My mother told me this was a good place to live," he said thoughtfully.

He held up one of his front paws. His feet were cold, for there was a draft coming from the stairs. Miss James's lap ought to be soft and warm.

Up he jumped and landed in the middle of her lap.

"Meow," he said, softly. Then he started to purr, for her lap was very soft and very warm. His purring grew louder and louder as his feet got warmer and warmer. He said, "Buzz-zz, buzz-zz, buzz-zz."

Miss James stroked his small gray head. "You seem to be a friendly little buzzie cat," she said gently. "A buzzie cat," she repeated. "Why, I think we'll call you Buzzie. You're a friendly little cat."

"I like you, too," Buzzie said.

He waited patiently for an answer. But Miss James did not say anything.

WHAT HAPPENED?

Buzzie could talk to his family. But he couldn't talk to Mr. James. He couldn't talk to Miss James. Why couldn't he talk to them? Buzzie tried to let them know his name. Finally they knew. How did Buzzie tell them?

THINK IT OVER

You can talk to people. But it isn't always easy to talk even when you have the words. Have you ever been in a new place? It's hard to talk then. You don't know anybody. You don't know what to say. What could you say to help people to know you?

Suppose a new boy comes to live in your neighborhood. Or maybe a new girl joins your class. They do not know anyone. How could you help them? What would you say?

UNIT THREE

MERRY TALES

THE UNHAPPY
TIGER

Georges Duplaix

One day a tiger saw two little goats who were playing just outside of the jungle.

"Look at the sweet little fellows," he thought. "Just what I want for breakfast."

The sly tiger crawled through the grass. All of a sudden he jumped on one of the little goats. But the other one ran away, crying with fright.

An old pelican who had seen the whole thing was angered by such cruelty. Of course he didn't dare to say anything to the tiger. He just watched him carry the goat into the jungle. He stood still and listened. After a long time he heard the tiger moan and cry in the most pitiful manner.

"What do I hear?" said the pelican. "He sounds heart-broken. The tiger is crying! He must be terribly sorry. . . . That shows you that the

From *Animal Stories* by Georges Duplaix, published by Simon and Schuster. Copyright, 1944, by Simon and Schuster, Inc. and Artists and Writers Guild, Inc.

107

meanest of the mean may have a soft spot after all. I'll go and talk to him. Maybe he will turn a new leaf and be a good tiger from now on."

Full of hope, the kind old pelican went into the jungle. Sure enough, he found the tiger in tears.

"Shame on you!" said the pelican to the tiger. "How could you be so cruel as to eat such a sweet little thing as that goat? He hadn't done anything to you! No wonder you feel guilty now! No wonder you're unhappy. Because I can tell that you are unhappy, aren't you?"

"Boo, hoo! Yes," said the tiger, "very unhappy."

"Well, it's all because you ate that little goat, that's why," said the pelican.

"No-o-o-o," said the tiger, crying harder than ever. "But *why*, oh, *why* didn't I catch both of the little goats? It would be so much fun to eat the other one now."

Then the pelican understood his mistake, and flew out of reach before it was too late.

"Ah," he said sadly, "tigers will be tigers!"

WHAT HAPPENED?

The tiger was very unhappy. At first the pelican was angry at the tiger. Why was the pelican angry?

Later the pelican felt sorry for the tiger. Then the tiger told the pelican why he was crying. Why was the tiger crying? How did the pelican feel then?

THINK IT OVER

The pelican said, "Tigers will be tigers." Maybe you have heard people say, "Boys will be boys," or "Girls will be girls." Sometimes they say it with a smile. Sometimes they say it with a sigh.

What kinds of things do boys and girls do which make grown-ups smile? What kinds of things make them sigh?

Suppose you've done something which makes a grown-up sigh. What should you say or do?

109

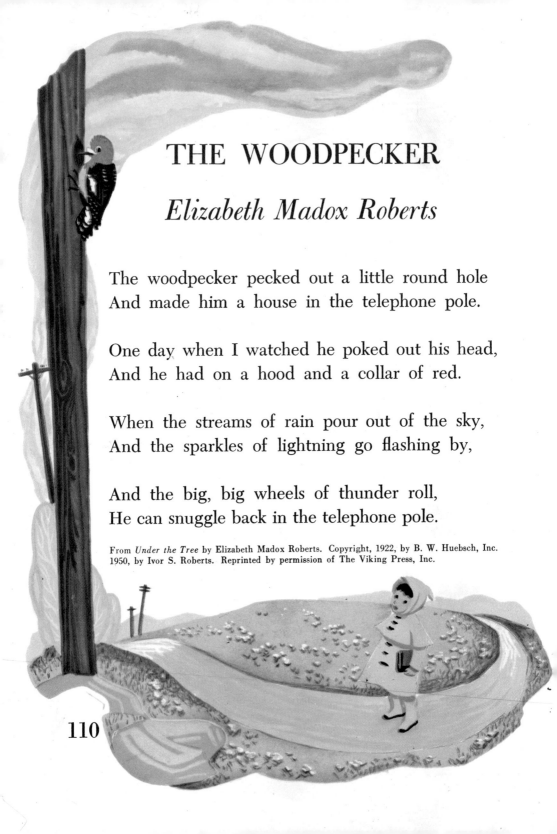

THE WOODPECKER

Elizabeth Madox Roberts

The woodpecker pecked out a little round hole
And made him a house in the telephone pole.

One day when I watched he poked out his head,
And he had on a hood and a collar of red.

When the streams of rain pour out of the sky,
And the sparkles of lightning go flashing by,

And the big, big wheels of thunder roll,
He can snuggle back in the telephone pole.

From *Under the Tree* by Elizabeth Madox Roberts. Copyright, 1922, by B. W. Huebsch, Inc. 1950, by Ivor S. Roberts. Reprinted by permission of The Viking Press, Inc.

THE HALF-CHICK

Spanish Folk Tale

There was once upon a time a black Spanish hen. She had a large family of chickens. They were all fat little birds except the youngest. He was not like his brothers and sisters. This one looked as if he had been cut in two. He had only one leg. He had only one wing. He had only one eye. And he had half a head and half a beak.

His mother was sad when she looked at him. She said, "My baby is only a half-chick. He can never grow up to be a tall rooster like his brothers. They will go out into the world and make their fortunes. But this poor little chick will always have to stay at home with his mother."

She called him Medio Pollito. This means "Half-Chick" in Spanish.

Now the mother hen soon found out that Half-

Adapted by Floy Winks DeLancey.

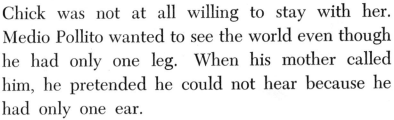

Chick was not at all willing to stay with her. Medio Pollito wanted to see the world even though he had only one leg. When his mother called him, he pretended he could not hear because he had only one ear.

When she took the family out for a walk in the fields, Medio Pollito would hop away by himself. Then he would hide in the corn.

One day he had been out for a long walk. When he came back he marched up to his mother. He gave a little hop and a kick. This was his way of walking. Then he cocked his one eye at her in a very bold way. He said, "Mother, I am tired of this life in the farmyard. There is nothing but a cornfield to look at. I am going to Madrid to see the king."

"To Madrid, Medio Pollito!" said his mother. "Why, you silly chick! It would be a long trip for a grown rooster. A poor little thing like you would be tired out before you had gone halfway. No. Stay at home with me. Some day, when you are bigger, we will go on a little trip together."

But Medio Pollito had made up his mind. He would not listen to his mother. He would not listen to his brothers and sisters.

"I want a fine place of my own," Medio Pollito said. "I want a fine place at the king's palace."

Away he stumped down the road that led to Madrid.

"Be sure you are kind to everyone you meet," called his mother. But he was in such a hurry to be off that he did not wait to answer her.

Later in the day, he went by a stream. The stream was filled with weeds and water plants.

"Oh, Medio Pollito!" the stream cried as the half-chick hopped along its bank. "Do come and help me. Please clear away these weeds."

"Help you?" said Medio Pollito. He shook his head and waved the few feathers in his half tail. "Do you think I have nothing to do but waste my time? You can help yourself. Don't trouble a busy person like me. I am off to Madrid to see the king." And hoppity-kick, hoppity-kick, away went Medio Pollito.

A little later he came to a fire that had been left in a wood. It was not burning well. It would soon be out.

"Oh, Medio Pollito," cried the fire, in a small voice. "In a few minutes I shall go out. Please put some sticks and dry leaves on me. Do help me or I shall die!"

113

"Help you?" said Medio Pollito. "I have other things to do. You can help yourself. Don't trouble me. I am off to Madrid to see the king." And hoppity-kick, hoppity-kick, away went Medio Pollito.

The next morning he went by a large tree. The wind was caught in its branches.

"Oh, Medio Pollito," called the wind, "do hop up here. Help me get free of this tree. I cannot get away."

"Help you?" said Medio Pollito. "I can't waste all my morning stopping here to help you. Don't trouble me. I am off to Madrid to see the king." And hoppity-kick, hoppity-kick, away went Medio Pollito.

Soon he could see the towers and roofs of Madrid. When he came into the town, he saw before him a big house. Soldiers stood before the gates. This must be the palace. He decided to hop up to the front gate and wait there until the king came out. But as he hopped past one of the back windows, the king's cook saw him.

114

"Here is the very thing I want," the cook said. "The king has just said that he wants chicken soup for dinner." The cook opened the window. He put out his arm and caught Medio Pollito. Then he popped him into the soup pot standing near the fire. Oh, how wet the water felt as it went over Medio Pollito's head!

"Water! Water!" he cried. "Do not wet me like this."

"Ah, Medio Pollito," said the water. "You would not help me when I was a stream in the field. Now you must be punished."

Then the fire began to burn Medio Pollito. He danced and hopped from one side of the pot to the other. He tried to get away from the heat. He cried out in pain.

"Fire! Fire! Do not burn me like this. It hurts."

"Ah, Medio Pollito," answered the fire. "You would not help me when I was dying in the wood. Now you must be punished."

When the pain was so great that Medio Pollito

thought he would die, the cook lifted up the lid of the soup pot. He wanted to see if the soup was ready for the king's dinner.

"Look here!" he cried. "This chicken is no good. It is burned to a cinder!"

He opened the window and threw Medio Pollito out into the street. But the wind caught Medio and whirled him through the air. Medio Pollito could hardly breathe. His heart beat against his side till he thought it would break.

"Oh, Wind," he called out, "if you hurry me along like this you will kill me. Do let me rest a minute, or —" But he was so out of breath that he could not finish his sentence.

"Ah, Medio Pollito," replied the wind, "when I was caught in the branches of the tree you would not help me. Now you are punished."

And he blew Medio Pollito over the roofs of the houses. At last they came to the highest church in the town. There the wind left Medio Pollito. He left him standing on top of the steeple on his one leg.

And there stands Medio Pollito to this very day. If you go to Madrid and walk through the streets, you will see him. He stands there on his one leg on the steeple of the church. His one wing droops at his side. And he looks sadly out of his one eye over the town.

WHAT HAPPENED?

Medio Pollito would not stay with his mother. He started out to see the king.

He passed by the stream, the fire, and the wind. Each one asked him for help. What did Medio Pollito say to them?

Finally he came to the royal palace. His welcome there was different from what he had expected. Who welcomed Medio Pollito? How did he welcome Medio Pollito?

The wind took Medio Pollito for a ride. And then the wind left Medio Pollito. Where did the wind leave him? Is there a Medio Pollito in your town?

THINK IT OVER

Have you ever heard of the Golden Rule? It is in the Bible. Do you know what it says? Treat other people the same way you want other people to treat you.

It is not easy to follow the Golden Rule all the time. Did Medio Pollito follow it? Can you think of times when it would be hard to follow the Golden Rule?

117

BOOTS AND HIS BROTHERS

Norse Legend

Once upon a time there were three brothers,
Peter, Paul, and John. John was the youngest.
He was called Boots.

Not far from their father's home was the king's
palace. By the side of the king's palace a great
oak tree had grown up. The tree was so big that
no light could shine through its branches.

The king said he would pay a great deal of
money to the man who could cut down the tree.
But no man had been able to do this. Every time
a chip flew from the oak, two chips grew in its
place.

The king also wanted a well, for there was no
well in the palace grounds. But no one could dig
a well there, because the palace stood on a big,

Adapted by Floy Winks DeLancey.

big rock. The king said that if any man could cut down the oak and dig a well, that man should have half the kingdom.

Many men came to try. But as they swung their axes, the oak grew larger and larger. When they tried to dig a well, the rock didn't get any softer, either.

One day the three brothers, Peter, Paul, and Boots, thought they would go to the palace. They would try to cut down the tree and dig the well.

The brothers had not gone far when they came to a big woods. The woods grew up over a steep hill. Away up among the trees, they could hear something chopping, chopping, chopping.

"I wonder what that is, chopping up on the hill," said Boots.

"A man chopping a tree down, of course," said the brothers.

"Still, I should like to see what it is," said Boots, and up the hill he went.

What do you think he saw there? He saw an axe that stood there chopping and chopping. It stood there all alone, chopping the trunk of a tree.

"Good day to you!" said Boots. "So you stand here alone and chop, do you?"

"Yes! I've stood here alone a long time, waiting for you," said the axe.

Boots pulled the axe from the tree and put it into his sack. Then he went back down the hill.

His brothers laughed when they saw him come back.

"Well, what did you see on the hill?" they asked.

"You were right. It was only an axe we heard," said Boots.

Soon they came to a rock hill. Away up on the rock they could hear something digging and digging.

"I wonder now," said Boots, "what is digging at the top of the rock hill."

"A woodpecker pecking on a tree, of course," said the brothers.

"Still, I should like to see what it is," said Boots, and up the rock he went.

What do you think he saw there? He saw a spade that stood there all alone, digging and digging.

"Good day to you!" said Boots. "So you stand here alone and dig, do you?"

"Yes! I've stood here alone a long time, waiting for you," said the spade.

Boots pulled the spade out of the rock and put it into his sack.

"Well," said his brothers. "What did you see on the rock?"

"Oh," said Boots, "nothing but a spade."

Soon the brothers came to a brook.

"I wonder," said Boots, "where all this water comes from."

"I wonder if you are right in your head," said Peter and Paul. "Where the brook comes from, indeed! Don't you know that water comes from springs in the earth?"

"Yes, but I should like to see for myself," said Boots.

He walked along the side of the brook for a long time. The brook was growing smaller and smaller. At last, what do you think he saw? Why,

a big walnut, and out of the walnut the water
trickled.

"Good day to you!" said Boots. "So you send
water into the brook all alone?"

"Yes! I have been here a long time, waiting for
you," said the walnut.

Boots picked some moss and stopped up the
hole in the walnut. Then he put the walnut into
his pocket and went back to his brothers.

"Well, now, Wonder Boy," said Peter and Paul,
"did you find where the brook water comes from?"

"Oh, after all, it was only a small hole it ran
out of," said Boots.

123

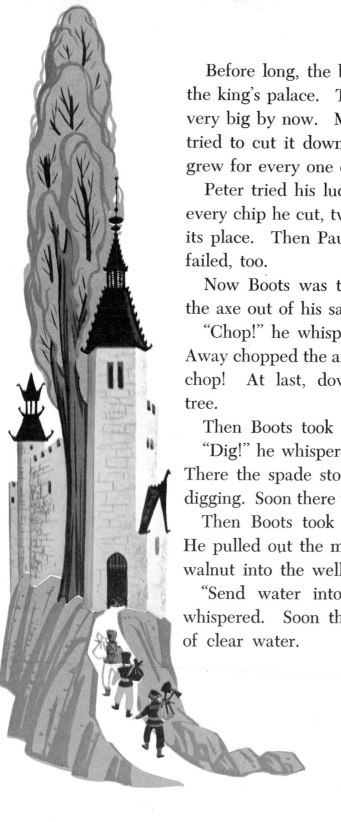

Before long, the brothers came to the king's palace. The oak tree was very big by now. Many people had tried to cut it down, and two chips grew for every one cut by an axe.

Peter tried his luck first. But for every chip he cut, two chips grew in its place. Then Paul tried. But he failed, too.

Now Boots was to try. He took the axe out of his sack.

"Chop!" he whispered to the axe. Away chopped the axe. Chop, chop, chop! At last, down fell the oak tree.

Then Boots took out his spade.

"Dig!" he whispered to the spade. There the spade stood, digging and digging. Soon there was a deep well.

Then Boots took out his walnut. He pulled out the moss and put the walnut into the well.

"Send water into the well!" he whispered. Soon the well was full of clear water.

Boots had done everything the king wanted. He had cut down the oak. He had dug a well in the rock, and the well was full of clear water. So half the kingdom was his.

"Well," said Peter and Paul. "Boots was right in his head after all when he began wondering."

WHAT HAPPENED?

Boots was curious. He was much more curious than his brothers. He heard a chopping noise on the hillside. He heard a digging noise also. He went to find out about them. What did he see each time?

Boots even wondered where the brook came from. He went to see it. His brothers laughed. Where did the brook come from?

Then they came to the palace of the king. The king said that he would give half of his kingdom to the man who could do two things. What were those two things? The brothers were not able to do them. But Boots did. How did he do them?

THINK IT OVER

"Curiosity killed a cat." Has anybody ever said that to you?

But curiosity is a good thing, too. Boots found it so. You can, too. When should you be curious?

125

THE SNAIL
AND THE MOUSE

Laura E. Richards

The Snail and the Mouse
Went round the house,
  Running a race together;
The riders were elves,
And proud of themselves,
  For neither weighed more than a feather.

The Snail went crawly, creepy, crawl,
  The Mouse went hoppety hop, sir;
But they came to a fence
That *was* so immense
  (Six inches!), they *had* to stop, sir!

"The Snail and the Mouse" from *I Have a Song to Sing You* by Laura E. Richards. Copyright, 1938, D. Appleton-Century Co., Inc. Reprinted by permission of the publishers, Appleton-Century-Crofts, Inc.

THE HARVEST ELVES

Wilfrid Thorley

The harvesters — they say themselves —
Are haunted by the harvest elves.

These elves — they say — as small as dolls
Have poppies for their parasols.

And, when you hear the swish of stalks,
It's elves a-sweeping their green walks.

And so when next a field you cross
And see the wheat-ears roll and toss,

Go quietly, and if you peep
Maybe you'll find an elf asleep

Inside a little hammock-bed,
Just as the harvesters have said.

From *The Happy Colt* by Wilfrid Thorley. Reprinted by permission of the publishers, Geo. G. Harrap and Co., Ltd.

THE TINDER BOX

Hans Christian Andersen

A soldier came marching along the road. One, two! One, two! He had a knapsack on his back and a sword at his side. On the road he met an old witch. She was so ugly that her lower lip hung right down on her chin.

She said, "Good evening, soldier! What a nice sword you have, and such a big knapsack. You shall have as much money as you want."

"Thank you kindly, old witch," said the soldier.

"Do you see that big tree?" asked the witch. "It is hollow inside. Climb to the top. There you will see a hole which will lead you right down under the tree. I can pull you up when you call."

"What am I to do under the tree?" asked the soldier.

Adapted by Floy Winks DeLancey.

128

"Get money," said the witch. "At the bottom of the tree you will find yourself in a wide hall. You will see three doors. The keys are in the doors.

"If you go into the first room you will see a big box in the middle of the floor. A dog is sitting on top of the box. He has eyes as big as saucers, but you needn't mind that. I will give you my blue apron. Put it on the floor. Put the dog on the apron. Then open the box and take out as much money as you want. It is copper money. If you like silver better, go into the next room.

"In the second room you will find a dog with eyes as big as millstones. Do not be afraid. Put him on the apron and take the money. If you like gold better than silver, go into the third room. The dog sitting on that box has eyes as big as a round tower. But don't let that worry you. Just put the dog on my apron and take as much gold as you want."

"That's not so bad," said the soldier. "But what do you want from me?"

"I only want you to bring me an old tinder box that is down there," said the witch.

The soldier climbed up the tree and slid down the hollow trunk. He found himself in the wide hall. Now he opened the first door. Ugh! There

sat the dog with eyes as big as saucers staring at him.

"Nice dog!" said the soldier. He put the dog on the witch's apron. He filled his pockets with pennies. Then he went into the next room. There sat the dog with eyes as big as millstones.

"Don't stare so hard," said the soldier. "You will get a pain in your big eyes!" Then he put the dog on the apron. When he saw the silver in the box, he threw away all the pennies. He filled his pockets and his knapsack with silver.

Then the soldier went into the third room. There sat the dog with eyes as big as a round tower, and they rolled around and around like wheels. What a sight!

"Good evening," said the soldier. He put the dog on the apron and opened the third chest. What a lot of gold! He could buy a whole city with it, and all the candy and toys in the world.

Now the soldier threw away all the silver and put gold in its place. Yes, he filled his pockets, his knapsack, his cap, and his boots so full that he could hardly walk. Then he put the dog back on the box and shut the door. He called up the tree, "Pull me up, old witch!"

"Have you got the tinder box?"

Oh, he had forgotten it. The soldier went back to get the box. Then the witch pulled him up.

"What do you want the tinder box for?" asked the soldier.

131

"That's no business of yours," said the witch. "You have your money. Give me the box."

"Tell me what you want with the tinder box," said the soldier, "or I will open it."

Just as he started to open the box, a clap of thunder rolled. The soldier looked up quickly. The old witch was gone and he never saw her again. The soldier put the tinder box in his pocket and walked to the town.

In the town, the soldier went to the best hotel. He ordered the best room and all the food he liked. He was a rich man now. The next day he bought new clothes. In the stores he heard the people talking about the king's daughter.

"She is a beautiful princess," the people all said.

"Where can I see the princess?" asked the soldier.

"You can't see her," the people said. "She lives in a great copper palace. No one but the king can go in and out. It has been said that she will marry a soldier, and the king does not like that."

The soldier led a happy life. He also gave away a lot of money to poor people, which was kind of him. But, alas, he spent so much money, and he gave away so much money that at last he had only two pennies left.

Then he had to move out of his fine rooms. He

132

had to take a tiny little room up under the roof. Nobody came to see him because there were so many stairs to climb. Finally he did not even have money to buy a candle for light.

One evening the soldier remembered the tinder box he had brought out of the hollow tree. He remembered that there was a little candle in the box. He took out the tinder box with the candle in it and struck fire. As the sparks flew out, the door of his room opened. There stood the dog with eyes as big as saucers.

"What do you wish, master?" said the dog.

The soldier was very surprised. "This is a fine tinder box if I can get what I want like this," he said to himself. To the dog he said, "Get me some money," and away the dog went. Soon he was back with a bag of pennies in his mouth.

The soldier found out that if he struck the tinder box once, the dog which sat on the box of pennies came. If he struck twice, the dog on the silver box came. And if he struck three times, the dog from the box of gold came.

Soon the soldier was rich again. Then he began to think about the princess.

"I would like to see the princess," he said. "Where is my tinder box?" Then he called for the dog with eyes as big as saucers.

133

"I know it is the middle of the night," said the soldier, "but I would like to see the princess, if only for a moment."

Before the soldier had time to think, the dog was back with the princess. She was fast asleep on the dog's back. The soldier thought she was beautiful. Then the dog ran back to the copper palace with the princess.

The next morning the princess told her parents about a dream she had had.

"I rode on a dog's back and I saw a soldier," she said.

The queen told the old lady-in-waiting to sit by the princess at night to see if this was really a dream. The next night the dog came to get the princess again. He took her and ran away as fast as he could. The old lady-in-waiting put on her

magic shoes and ran just as fast behind them.
When she saw that they went into a large house,
she thought, "Now I know where it is." She made
a big cross on the gate with chalk. Then she went
back to the palace.

Soon the dog came back with the princess.
When he saw the chalk mark on the gate, he took
some chalk, too, and made crosses on all the gates
in the town.

Early the next morning the king, the queen, and
the lady-in-waiting went to find the house where
the princess had been.

"There it is," said the king, when he saw the
first door with the cross on it.

"No, my dear, it is there," said the queen, who
saw another door with a cross on it.

"But there is one! And there is another!" they
all cried out. They soon saw that they could not
find the right gate.

Now the queen took her big gold scissors and
cut up a large piece of cloth into small pieces.
Then she made a little bag which she filled with

135

grain. She tied the bag to the back of the princess. When that was done she cut a little hole in the bag. Now the grain would drop out and leave a trail wherever the princess went.

That night the dog came again. He took the princess to the soldier. The soldier was so much in love with the princess by now that he wanted to marry her. Now the dog did not see how the grain dropped out all along the way. In the morning the king and the queen saw where their daughter had been. They had the soldier put in prison.

There he lay. The prison was dark and cold. One day they said to him, "Tomorrow you are to die." This was sad news for the soldier. He did not even have his tinder box with him.

The next morning he saw a boy go by the prison. The soldier called to the boy.

"Boy!" the soldier said, "if you will run to the house where I used to live and bring me my tinder box, you shall have a penny."

The boy was glad to earn a penny. He brought the box and gave it to the soldier.

When it was time for the soldier to die, he climbed the ladder to the platform. The king and queen sat upon a beautiful throne nearby. The soldier turned to them and asked if he could smoke a pipe. After all, it would be his last in this world. The king said, "Yes."

Out came the tinder box and the soldier struck fire — once, twice, three times. In a wink all three dogs were there — the one with eyes like saucers, the one with eyes like millstones, and the one whose eyes were as big as a round tower.

"Save me!" cried the soldier.

The dogs rushed toward the king and toward the queen and toward all the people. Everyone was very frightened. The people shouted, "Oh, good soldier, call off the dogs. You shall be our king and marry the beautiful princess!"

Then they took the soldier to the copper palace while the dogs danced along in front of him and shouted "Hurrah!"

The princess was happy to leave the copper palace and become queen. At the wedding, the dogs had seats at the table where they all sat looking with their big wide eyes.

WHAT HAPPENED?

It was just as the witch said. Each dog in the hall under the tree was more terrible than the one before. The third dog was the worst of all. What kind of eyes did each dog have?

Long ago people used a tinder box to help them make fire. What happened to the witch when the soldier opened the tinder box?

When the soldier's money was gone, the dog with eyes as big as saucers helped him to get more money. How did the soldier call the dog? What did the dog do to help?

Later, the dog brought the princess to the soldier. Once the lady-in-waiting chased after him. The dog went into a house. The lady-in-waiting made a cross on the gate with chalk. But the next day the king and queen could not find the house. Why couldn't they find the house?

The queen thought of another way to find where the dog went. What did she do?

It looked as if the soldier was going to die. His tinder box was back in his house. He was in jail. How did he get the box?

THINK IT OVER

The soldier had the tinder box to help him when he was in trouble. Boys and girls have their parents to help them. But of course they don't expect Father or Mother to take care of every trouble every time. What kinds of trouble should parents help with? What kinds of trouble should boys and girls take care of by themselves?

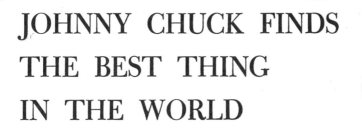

JOHNNY CHUCK FINDS THE BEST THING IN THE WORLD

Thornton Burgess

Old Mother West Wind had stopped to talk with the slender fir tree.

"I've just come across the green meadows," said Old Mother West Wind, "and there I saw the best thing in the world."

Striped Chipmunk was sitting under the slender fir tree and he couldn't help hearing what Old Mother West Wind said. "The best thing in the world — now what can that be?" thought Striped Chipmunk. "Why, it must be heaps and heaps of nuts and acorns! I'll go and find it."

So Striped Chipmunk started down the lone little path through the wood as fast as he could run. Pretty soon he met Peter Rabbit.

"Where are you going in such a hurry, Striped Chipmunk?" asked Peter Rabbit.

"Down in the green meadows to find the best thing in the world," replied Striped Chipmunk, and ran faster.

"The best thing in the world," said Peter Rabbit, "why, that must be a great pile of carrots and cabbage. I think I'll go and find it."

So Peter Rabbit started down the lone little path through the wood as fast as he could go after Striped Chipmunk.

As they passed the great hollow tree Bobby Coon put his head out. "Where are you going in such a hurry?" asked Bobby Coon.

"Down in the green meadows to find the best thing in the world!" shouted Striped Chipmunk and Peter Rabbit, and both began to run faster.

"The best thing in the world," said Bobby Coon to himself, "why, that must be a whole field of sweet milky corn. I think I'll go and find it."

So Bobby Coon climbed down out of the great hollow tree and started down the lone little path through the wood as fast as he could go after

140

Striped Chipmunk and Peter Rabbit, for there is nothing that Bobby Coon likes to eat as well as milky corn.

At the edge of the wood they met Jimmy Skunk.

"Where are you going in such a hurry?" asked Jimmy Skunk.

"Down in the green meadows to find the best thing in the world!" shouted Striped Chipmunk and Peter Rabbit and Bobby Coon. Then they all tried to run faster.

"The best thing in the world," said Jimmy Skunk. "Why, that must be packs and packs of beetles!" And for once in his life Jimmy Skunk began to hurry down the lone little path after Striped Chipmunk and Peter Rabbit and Bobby Coon.

They were all running so fast that they didn't see Reddy Fox until he jumped out of the long grass and asked:

"Where are you going in such a hurry?"

"To find the best thing in the world!" shouted Striped Chipmunk and Peter Rabbit and Bobby

Coon and Jimmy Skunk, and each did his best to run faster.

"The best thing in the world," said Reddy Fox to himself, "why, that must be a whole pan of tender young chickens, and I must have them."

So away went Reddy Fox, as fast as he could run, down the lone little path after Striped Chipmunk, Peter Rabbit, Bobby Coon, and Jimmy Skunk.

By and by they all came to the house of Johnny Chuck.

"Where are you going in such a hurry?" asked Johnny Chuck.

"To find the best thing in the world," shouted Striped Chipmunk and Peter Rabbit and Bobby Coon and Jimmy Skunk and Reddy Fox.

"The best thing in the world," said Johnny Chuck. "Why, I don't know of anything better than my own little home and the warm sunshine and the beautiful blue sky."

So Johnny Chuck stayed at home and played all day among the flowers with the merry little breezes of Old Mother West Wind and was as happy as could be.

But all day long Striped Chipmunk and Peter Rabbit and Bobby Coon and Jimmy Skunk and Reddy Fox ran this way and ran that way over the green meadows, trying to find the best thing in the world. The sun was very, very warm and they ran so far and they ran so fast that they were very, very hot and tired, and still they hadn't found the best thing in the world.

143

When the long day was over they started up the
lone little path past Johnny Chuck's house to their
own homes. They didn't hurry now for they were
so very, very tired. And they were cross — oh, so
cross! Striped Chipmunk hadn't found a single
nut. Peter Rabbit hadn't found so much as the
leaf of a cabbage. Bobby Coon hadn't found the
tiniest bit of sweet milky corn. Jimmy Skunk
hadn't seen a single beetle. Reddy Fox hadn't
heard so much as the peep of a chicken. And all
were as hungry as hungry could be.

Halfway up the lone little path they met Old
Mother West Wind going to her home behind the
hill. "Did you find the best thing in the world?"
asked Old Mother West Wind.

"No!" shouted Striped Chipmunk and Peter
Rabbit and Bobby Coon and Jimmy Skunk and
Reddy Fox all together.

144

"Johnny Chuck has it," said Old Mother West Wind. "It is being happy with the things you have and not wanting things which someone else has. And it is called Con-tent-ment."

WHAT HAPPENED?

Old Mother West Wind found it first. It was the best thing in the world. She told the fir tree about it. Striped Chipmunk tried to find it. What did he look for? What did Peter Rabbit think it was? What did Bobby Coon look for? Jimmy Skunk thought he knew. What did he look for? What did Reddy Fox think it was?

Only Johnny Chuck really knew what it was. He had found the best thing in the world long ago. Just where did Johnny Chuck find it? Old Mother West Wind had a name for it. What did she call the best thing in the world?

THINK IT OVER

"Count your blessings" is an old, old saying. It means thinking of all the things you have to make you happy. Some boys are glad they have dogs. Some girls are glad they have nice clothes. All boys and girls are glad they have good friends. What is the best thing in the world for you? How many blessings can you count?

145

LIONS AND DRAGONS

Dorothy Aldis

Snap-Dragons and Dande-Lions
Are not so very wild —
I never yet saw one forget
And try to hurt a child.

A Dande-Lion never ROARS
Not even once, for fun;
Nor waves a tail with angry wail —
Because he hasn't one!

A Snap-Dragon will never snap
No matter how he feels,
Except to try to catch a fly
To brighten up his meals.

From *Everything and Anything* by Dorothy Aldis. Copyright, 1925,
by G. P. Putnam's Sons.

THE FUNNY THING

Wanda Gág

It was a beautiful day in the mountains. The sun was playing hide-and-seek among the fluffy, floating clouds, and the air was soft and warm.

Bobo, the good little man of the mountains, was waiting for the birds and animals to come. To come for what do you suppose? To come for food — because at the door of his mountain cave, Bobo had many good things for them to eat.

He had nut cakes for the fuzzy-tailed squirrels. He had seed puddings for the pretty fluttering birds. He had cabbage salads for the long-eared rabbits. He had tiny cheeses — no bigger than cherries — and these were for the little mice.

Now on this beautiful sunny day, there came a Funny Thing which Bobo had never seen before. It looked something like a dog and also a little

Reprinted by permission of Coward-McCann, Inc., publishers.

like a giraffe, and from the top of its head to the
tip of its curled tail, there was a row of beautiful
blue points.

"Good morning," said Bobo. "And what kind
of an animal are you?"

"I'm not an animal," said the Funny Thing.
"I'm an *aminal*!"

Bobo was about to say that there was no such
word as *aminal*, when the Funny Thing looked
around fiercely and cried, "And what have you
for a hungry *aminal* to eat?"

"Oh," said Bobo, "here are some lovely nut
cakes. I also have some fine seed puddings. This
cabbage salad is very nice — and I'm sure you'd
like these little cheeses."

But the Funny Thing turned away and said, "I never heard of such silly food! No *aminal* would eat those things. Haven't you any dolls today?"

"Dolls!" cried Bobo in surprise.

"Certainly," said the Funny Thing. "And very good they are — dolls."

"To eat?" cried Bobo, opening his eyes very wide at such an idea.

"To eat, of course," said the Funny Thing, smacking his lips. "And very good they are — dolls."

"But it is not kind to eat up little children's dolls," said Bobo. "I should think it would make them very unhappy."

"So it does," said the Funny Thing, smiling pleasantly, "but very good they are — dolls."

"And don't the children cry when you take away their dolls?" asked Bobo.

"Don't they, though!" said the Funny Thing with a cheerful grin. "But very good they are — dolls."

Tears rolled down Bobo's face as he thought of the Funny Thing going around eating up dear little children's dolls.

149

"But perhaps you take only naughty children's dolls," he said, brightening up.

"No, I take them specially from good children," said the Funny Thing gleefully, "and *very* good they are — good children's dolls!"

"Oh, what shall I do," thought Bobo, as he walked back and forth, back and forth. He was trying to think of a plan to make this naughty *aminal* forget to eat dolls.

At last he had an idea!

So he said to the Funny Thing, "What a lovely tail you have!"

150

The Funny Thing smiled and wriggled his tail with a pleased motion.

"And those pretty black eyebrows," Bobo continued.

The Funny Thing looked down modestly and smiled even more.

"But most wonderful of all is that row of blue points down your back," said Bobo.

The Funny Thing was so pleased at this that he rolled foolishly on the ground and smiled very hard.

Then Bobo, who was really a wise old man, said to the Funny Thing, "I suppose you are so beautiful because you eat a great many jum-jills?"

The Funny Thing had never heard of them.

"Jum-jills?" he asked eagerly. "What is a jum-jill — is it a kind of doll?"

"Oh, no," said Bobo. "Jum-jills are funny little cakes which make blue points more beautiful, and little tails grow into big ones."

151

Now the Funny Thing was very vain and there was nothing he would rather have had than a very long tail and bigger and more beautiful blue points. So he cried, "Oh, please, dear kind man, give me many jum-jills!"

"Very well," said Bobo. "Sit down under this tree and wait for me."

The Funny Thing was all smiles and did as he was told, while Bobo went into his cozy little home, which was like a sort of tunnel under the mountain.

First he had to go through his little bedroom. Next he came to his study and finally reached the kitchen, where he usually made up the food for the birds and animals.

Now he took a big bowl, into which he put:

> seven nut cakes
> five seed puddings
> two cabbage salads
> and fifteen little cheeses.

He mixed them with a spoon and rolled them into little round balls.

These little balls were jum-jills.

154

He put them all on a plate and carried them out to the Funny Thing, who was still waiting under the tree.

"Here are your jum-jills," said Bobo, as he handed the plate to the Funny Thing.

The Funny Thing ate one and said, "And very good they are — jum-jills."

Then he ate another and said, "And very good they are — jum-jills." And so on until he had eaten them all up. "And *very* good they are — jum-jills," he said with a smack of his lips, after they were all gone.

Then the Funny Thing went home, but the next day he came back for more jum-jills. His

tail was already a little longer, his blue points were beginning to grow, and he looked very happy indeed.

Every day the Funny Thing came back for more jum-jills. He came for a long, long time and each day his tail was a little longer. But on the twentieth day his tail had grown so long that he couldn't move about much. So he chose a nice big mountain and sat on the very top of it.

Every day Bobo sent birds to carry jum-jills to the Funny Thing, and as the Funny Thing's tail grew longer and longer he curled it contentedly about his mountain.

His only joy in life was his beautiful blue-pointed tail, and by and by the only words he ever said were: "And very good they are — jum-jills!"

So of course he ate no more dolls and we have kind old Bobo to thank for that.

WHAT HAPPENED?

Bobo took care of the birds and animals. He fed them nut cakes, seed puddings, cabbage salads. He even had small cheeses for the mice.

But the Funny Thing was different. What funny name did he call himself? Bobo wouldn't feed the Funny Thing what he had always eaten. What had the Funny Thing always eaten?

Bobo fixed him something special. How did Bobo make the "jum-jills"?

The Funny Thing liked "jum-jills." You could tell by what happened to his blue points and tail. What happened to them?

THE OLD TURTLE

Marie Hall Ets

If you want to live to be one-
Hundred-and-sixty or -sixty-one,
Ask the old turtle how it is done.
But ask him too: Has it been any fun
To live to be one-
Hundred-and-sixty or -sixty-one?

From *Beasts and Nonsense* by Marie Hall Ets. Copyright, 1952, by
Marie Hall Ets. Reprinted by permission of The Viking Press, Inc.

UNIT FOUR

CHILDREN'S THEATER

PLAYMAKING

FOR EVERYONE

Floy Winks DeLancey

MAKE-BELIEVE
WITHOUT
WORDS

Tom is acting out a Mother Goose rhyme. But he is not saying the rhyme. Acting without words is called pantomime.

Can you tell which Mother Goose rhymes these children are acting out?

Think of other Mother Goose rhymes to act in pantomime. Divide your class into teams. Let the teams take turns acting out a Mother Goose rhyme in pantomime. See if the other teams can guess the names of the rhymes.

Can you act out something an animal does? How would you walk if you were pretending to be a bear? a cat? an elephant? Let the class guess what animal you are pretending to be.

MORE MAKE-BELIEVE WITHOUT WORDS

Here are some ideas for acting without words. Try acting them out. Then think of other things to do in pantomime.

1. A cowboy rides a bucking horse.

2. A pilot checks his plane before starting on a trip.

3. A mother tries to hang clothes on the line when the wind is blowing.

4. The soldier puts the dog with eyes as big as saucers on the apron and fills his pockets with pennies.

MAKE-BELIEVE
WITH WORDS

Below are some make-believes to do with words. What do you think the people in these pretends would say first? What would they say next?

Talk about the make-believes in class. Then choose pupils to act the parts with words and action.

1. Two space cadets land on Mars. It is their first visit.

2. A little girl is lost from her mother in a big store. A worker in the store helps her.

3. The Pelican talks to the Unhappy Tiger.

4. A cowboy and an Indian meet on a mountain trail and talk about hunting.

5. Two boys talk about their fishing trip.

6. A salesman tries to sell a housewife something she does not want.

MAKING A STORY
INTO A PLAY

Do you remember the story of "The Half-Chick"? You will find it on page 111. Here is a play made from this story.

When you read the play aloud, the parts in italics, *like this*, are not to be read. We call these parts of a play the "stage directions." Stage directions tell the actors what to do while they speak the parts. They also tell what the stage looks like.

The names of characters should not be read aloud, either.

The following play has two "scenes." That part of the story takes place in one and part of it in another. When you act it in class, you can divide the front of your classroom into two parts. Have one scene take place in one part and the other scene take place in the other part.

Remember to speak clearly so that everyone can hear and understand what you are saying.

LITTLE HALF-CHICK

Dramatization by Floy Winks DeLancey

SCENE 1

Half-Chick runs or hops onto the stage. His Mother and Two Brothers are chasing him.

MOTHER. Half-Chick! Half-Chick! Come back. cannot go into the world alone.

HALF-CHICK (*stops and turns to his mother*). I do nt to stay at home. Nothing ever happens there. I want to visit the King at the palace on the hill.

MOTHER (*putting her arm around Half-Chick's shoulders*). What an idea, little one! We do not have fine clothes for the palace. You must stay at home with me and work in the garden.

HALF–CHICK. No, Mother. You said that my brothers could go into the world to seek their fortunes.

FIRST BROTHER. But Half-Chick, you are not strong. You can't seek your fortune.

HALF–CHICK. I may be only a little half-chick, but I want to see the world, too. And you can't keep me from it.

SECOND BROTHER. What a temper you have, little one! Come, go home now with Mother.

MOTHER. Come, Half-Chick.

HALF–CHICK (*hopping up and down on one leg angrily*). No! Go away and leave me alone. I hate you all! I hate you!

MOTHER (*shaking her head sadly*). Come, my big boys. (*She turns to the two brothers.*) We will go back home. Perhaps when he is all alone in the woods, Half-Chick will see that we were right.

The Mother and Two Brothers exit right. Half-Chick watches them leave, then turns to left of stage. He sees a Brook at back of stage. This may be played by a child lying on the floor. Half-Chick talks to himself.

HALF-CHICK. Stay at home, indeed! I don't want to work!

BROOK. Oh, Half-Chick! Please help me. I have been waiting for someone to come along. See how the weeds and plants have choked me. Please tear them away, or I will never be able to travel again. Please!

HALF-CHICK (*crossing to Brook and looking down*). Help you, indeed! I don't care whether you ever travel again or not. I am the one who wants to travel.

BROOK. Please help me!

HALF-CHICK. Do you think I have nothing to do but waste my time on you? Help yourself if you want help. I am on my way to Madrid to see the King.

Half-Chick hops on. Brook calls after him.

BROOK. If you won't help me, please help the Fire. Listen! He is calling to you. Hurry!

FIRE (*voice calling from rear of stage*). Help! Help! Unless you put some dry sticks on me, I will die. Half-Chick, help me!

HALF–CHICK (*sits down to rest*). Help you, indeed! I have other things to do. After I rest for a minute, I am hopping off to Madrid to see the King. Die for all I care, Mr. Fire.
Half-Chick sits rubbing his one leg. Fire continues to call for help. After a minute, Fire's voice dies away. Half-Chick rises and starts to hop on.

WIND. Help!
Half-Chick stops and looks up. Wind is caught in a tree. Wind can be sitting on top of a kitchen stool, pretending the stool is a tree.

HALF–CHICK (*doubling over with laughter*). Well, look who's here! Old Mr. Wind himself caught in the branches of a tree. What a joke!

WIND. It's no joke to me. Please, Half-Chick, hop up here and help me get free of these

166

branches. I cannot get away by myself.

HALF–CHICK. It's not my fault you're caught up there. Don't bother me, for I am off to Madrid to visit the King. Good-by, silly Wind! (*Half-Chick hops off stage left.*)

SCENE 2

The kitchen of the palace. Half-Chick is just about to knock at the door when it opens and out steps the Cook.

HALF–CHICK. Hello there, Cook. I've come to see the King. Which way do I go?

COOK. Well, am I in luck! You are just what I want, for the King has just sent word that he wants some chicken soup for supper. Into the water you go, little chick.

167

The Cook pushes him toward a large pot sitting on the table. Water is sitting under the table, with Fire by his side. You can pretend that the table is a stove. Of course the Cook can't really put the boy who plays Half-Chick into the iron pot. But he can shove him under the table and you can pretend the rest.

HALF–CHICK (*trying to fight as the Cook shoves him under the table*). Water, Water, don't wet me like this. Please help me!

WATER. Did you help me when I was a little brook back in the forest? Now you must be punished for treating me as you did.

HALF–CHICK. Ouch! The water is hot! Fire, Fire, don't burn. Help me, please!

FIRE. Did you help me when I was dying away in the wood?

HALF–CHICK. Well, it is I who am dying now. Help!

COOK (*looking into the pot*). This little chicken is really not fit for the King. It is burned to a cinder. I'll just throw it out the window.

The Cook pulls Half-Chick out from under the table and shoves him aside. The Wind runs onto the stage and grabs Half-Chick by the arm.

COOK. See how quickly the wind blew little Half-Chick away. Strong, big wind.

HALF–CHICK. Wind, Wind, you will kill me if you hurry along like this. Do please let me rest a minute. Help me, please!

WIND. Did you help me when I was caught in the branches of the big oak tree? Now I cannot help you. (*He continues to pull Half-Chick across the stage.*)

HALF–CHICK. But where are you taking me? We are going so very fast. I am dizzy.

WIND. I am taking you to the tallest church steeple in the town. There you will stand forever on your one leg and tell the people which way the wind blows.

The Wind shoves Half-Chick onto a chair or table. As the play ends, Half-Chick stands there on one leg, looking sadly at the class while the Wind runs round and round him.

PLAYMAKING
OF YOUR OWN

Here are two short animal stories written long ago by a man named Aesop. After you read each story, think about how many characters the play will need. What would you plan next? You may want to choose children for the parts and see how well they can act out the stories.

THE DOG IN THE MANGER

Aesop

One day a dog went into a barn. He lay down on some hay in the manger. In a little while an ox came into the barn. The ox was hungry and wanted to eat the hay.

"Please get out of my manger," the ox said politely. "I want to eat my dinner."

"No!" said the dog. "Go away and leave me alone."

"Do you like to eat hay?" asked the ox.

"Of course not," said the dog. "I like meat. Dogs never eat hay."

The ox said, "Then please let me eat it. I like hay."

The dog snarled. "No!" he said. "You shall not have the hay. Go away or I will bite you. Gr-r-r!"

The ox moved back and shook his head sadly. "You are a mean dog," he said. "You do not want to eat the hay yourself, but you will not let me have it. What a selfish dog you are!"

171

THE FOX AND THE CROW

Aesop

Once a black crow was sitting in a tree. She had some cheese in her mouth. A fox came along and saw the cheese. He thought the cheese looked delicious.

The fox went up to the tree and called to the crow. He told her how beautiful she was. He said he was sure she had a beautiful singing voice, too. He asked her to sing a song for him.

The crow liked to be told that she was beautiful. She wanted to show off her beautiful voice, too. She opened her mouth to sing, and the cheese fell to the ground.

The fox grabbed the cheese and gobbled it up. Then he told the crow that he really didn't want to hear her sing. "I think you are very ugly," the fox said. "But I DID want your cheese."

The crow decided that she had been very silly. "I should not have believed what that sly fox told me," she said. "He was only flattering me to get what he wanted."

A REAL PLAY

You have done pantomiming and you have written plays. Now you are ready to present a real theater play. See how well you can use what you have learned.

THE BREMEN TOWN MUSICIANS

Dramatization by Floy Winks DeLancey

Characters

Donkey	Dog	Robbers (*offstage*)
Cat	Rooster	

Scene: A country road, with a house at one end of the stage, right. The Cat is asleep center back of stage by side of road.

As the curtain rises, the Donkey enters from left.

DONKEY. Ho, hum. I want to go to Bremen Town. But I am lonesome all by myself. (*He looks back over his shoulder, offstage.*) Here comes a little dog. Maybe he will go with me. *Dog enters from left; stops when he sees the Donkey.*

DOG. Hello. What are you doing here?

DONKEY. And what are you doing here? This is a lonely road.

DOG. I'm on my way to Bremen Town. I hear they have good dog biscuits there.

DONKEY. Just where I'm bound for, too. Shall we travel together?

They go on a few steps. Dog sees the Cat and moves over to her side. Cat wakes up and jumps away.

DOG. What have we here? A cat! Strange company for a dog.

DONKEY. What are you doing here, Cat?

CAT. I was on my way to Bremen Town. I hear there are fat mice there. But I was tired traveling all alone and stopped to take a nap — a cat nap, you know!

DONKEY. Just where we're bound for, too. Would you like to join us?

CAT. That I would. If — (*She looks at Dog.*) if Mr. Dog doesn't care.

DOG. The more the merrier, I always say. I'm looking for dog biscuits and you're looking for mice. We won't bother each other.

DONKEY. Good! It's settled, then. Come, let's be on our way.

175

DOG. Cat had a good idea. Why don't we rest here for a moment?

All sit down. Dog and Donkey go to sleep. Cat licks her paws. Rooster enters from left. Cat shakes Dog and Donkey to waken them. Dog stretches. Donkey brays.

CAT. See, my friends? More company. A nice fat rooster. Does that look good to you, Dog?

DOG (*rises and looks at Rooster, who has stopped to stare at other animals*). A nice fat rooster, I'll be bound. But no. It's dog biscuit I want.

DONKEY. And where are you bound for, Chanticleer? This is a lonely road.

ROOSTER. I'm on my way to Bremen Town. Fine bugs and worms they have there, I understand. But this is a lonely road. And robbers live in yonder woods, I'm told.

CAT. Robbers, eh? Join us, then. We're all on our way to Bremen Town. And against the four of us, what chance do robbers have?

ROOSTER (*crows happily*). Four of us on the way to Bremen Town. Hurrah! Let's go! But let's keep together now. I heard strange sounds in the woods.

DONKEY. Strange sounds?

They all listen. There is a murmur of voices offstage.

DOG. Strange sounds? From that house down the road, no doubt.

CAT. Strange sounds? It doesn't sound like mice. But it might be. Let's creep up close and see.

ROOSTER. It doesn't sound like bugs and worms, either.

They all creep slowly toward house at right of stage.

DONKEY. I'll just look in the window here and see. (*He tries to look in window.*) Alas! The window is too high!

DOG. Down, Donkey, on all fours. When I stand on top of you, I'll be able to see.

Donkey kneels; Dog climbs on top but cannot see in the window.

CAT. Look! Here's a ladder! Wait where you are. I'll climb the ladder and jump onto your back, Dog. Then I can see. (*Cat climbs ladder, leans over shoulder of Dog, but cannot see in.*)

ROOSTER. It's my turn now. Down, Cat. I'll climb the ladder. Once on top, I can fly up to the window and see what makes the noise.

Cat climbs down ladder; Rooster climbs up ladder, and looks in window. He turns to whisper; noise in house increases to shouts and screams. When noise dies down, Rooster says:

ROOSTER. Robbers, friends! It's the robbers within. Food on the table and money piled all around.

DOG. Food! And I'm so hungry. Any dog biscuits there?

CAT. Any mice?

DONKEY. Money, did you say?

ROOSTER. Aye, money — sacks of it. And

roast chicken and cake and lemon pie and ice cream and candy and —

DOG. Hush! I'm starved. Even lemon pie is better than nothing. How can we get in?

DONKEY. Get in? I don't know —

CAT. Don't act like a donkey! Get in, indeed! We must be quiet so they won't hear a sound.

DONKEY. If we could just scare all those men away — then we'd have the food and the money, too.

CAT. I'll meow. Dog, you bark. Rooster, you crow. Donkey, bray as loud as ever you can. We'll make such a noise every man will run. Ready, get set, go!

Cat meows; Dog barks; Rooster crows; Donkey brays.

179

ROBBERS (*offstage*). What's that? What's that?

Sounds of scurrying and running. Animals laugh loudly.

ROOSTER. Such a scurry! See them run! Now we'll go in. We'll eat. We'll drink.

CAT. We'll sleep, too, I vow. We'll sleep the whole night through.

DOG (*laughing again*). What music we made, eh?

DONKEY. When we get to Bremen Town, my friends, we can form a singing group.

ROOSTER. We'll give concerts.

CAT. We'll be rich.

DOG. We'll travel everywhere. And with the money inside there we'll buy dog biscuits —

DONKEY. Yes, and nice rich hay, too —

ROOSTER. And grain will make me as happy as bugs and worms.

CAT. A tasty can of cat food now, and you can have all the mice in the world.

They enter the house, arm in arm, singing.

CURTAIN

180

SOME POEMS

FOR PLAYMAKING

Often it is fun to act out a poem. You will need to choose characters to take the parts and talk about what they should say. You may also want to talk about what action there will be in the play, and how many scenes.

The first poem has six characters — three jolly gentlemen and their three horses. One pupil may read the poem aloud while the six characters act it out in pantomime. Or the class may read the poem aloud while the poem is acted out.

On page 184 you will find ideas to use in acting out the second poem.

THE HUNTSMEN

Walter de la Mare

Three jolly gentlemen,
  In coats of red,
Rode their horses
  Up to bed.

Three jolly gentlemen
  Snored till morn,
Their horses champing
  The golden corn.

Three jolly gentlemen,
  At break of day,
Came clitter-clatter down the stairs
  And galloped away.

THREE OLD CATTLEMEN

Monica Shannon

Three Old Cattlemen
  Sleep under a tree.
Up goes a lizard,
  Down comes a bee.
Up goes a chipmunk
  And gives the tree a shake —
Three Old Cattlemen
  Are wide awake.

Three Old Cattlemen
  Run for their lives.
"Things are after us!"
  They tell their wives.
"What kind of things?"
  The wives inquire —
Three Old Cattlemen
  Snore by the fire.

From *Goose Grass Rhymes* by Monica Shannon. Copyright, 1930, by Doubleday & Company, Inc.

How many characters are there in the second poem?

What can you use for the tree?

How will the lizard act?

What noise will the bee make? What noise will the chipmunk make?

How many scenes will you need? Could you have the tree in one corner of the room and the wives' house in another corner?

What kind of costumes might the Three Old Cattlemen wear?

A POEM AND A SONG FOR ACTING

You have all used music for dancing. Poetry is like music. You can dance to poetry, too. Read the poem on the next page. Try to think how you would act the poem in pantomime. Then listen to the song. Plan a dance to go with the poem and the song. You will find some ideas to help you on page 187.

RING-A-RING O' FAIRIES

Madeleine Nightingale

Ring-a-ring o' fairies,
Pixies, sprites, and elves,
Dancing with a little boy
As nimble as themselves.
Charm a sleepy song-thrush
To sing a fairy tune.
Was ever such a pretty dance
Seen beneath the moon?

From *Fifty New Poems for Children* by Madeleine Nightingale.
Reprinted by permission of Basil Blackwell & Mott Limited,
publishers.

FAIRIES DANCING

Quickly POLISH FOLK DANCE

Fair - y   tunes   ring - ing   and
Fair - y   folk   whirl - ing   and

fai - ry folk   danc-ing   on   lawn and in
fai - ry feet   sway-ing   Oh!   hear the wild

hol - low   Their   sil - vry wings   are
mus - ic   of   fair - y   pip - ers

glanc-ing   Hey! the moon   shin- ing,   and
play- ing   Fast - er elves   fast - er   a -

ho!   for spring time   weath-er   skip-ping now and
lack! The Moon's de - clin-ing   Fair - y   folk must

dip- ping   they   trip   it   all   to - get-her.
van - ish   a - way! The dawn is   shin-ing.

From *Songs and Pictures, Third Book*, by Robert Foresman. Reprinted by permission of the American Book Company, publishers.

Getting ready to act out the poem and song:

1. Make a big yellow moon.
2. Choose someone to hold the moon.
3. Choose someone for the boy.
4. Choose someone for the song-thrush.
5. Choose some fairies, pixies, sprites, and elves.

Acting out the poem and song: A child may hold the big yellow moon high over his head.

The fairies, pixies, sprites, and elves dance in a circle with the boy. While they are dancing, the song-thrush and all the children who are not in the play may sing the song.

At the end of the song the moon goes down and all the characters skip away, leaving the boy alone. Then the boy may pretend to go to sleep.

PLAYMAKING IDEAS

Have you had fun making plays? Below is a list of other stories in your book which you can use for playmaking.

JOHNNY CHUCK. Make a list of the animals that went to the green meadow. Use the conversation in the story for your dialogue.

DANNY'S WISH COMES TRUE. This story begins in Danny's city home. What other places are there in the story? Choose one place and act out the things that happen there.

THE FUNNY THING. Choose one pupil to be Bobo and one to be The Funny Thing. Have them talk together about good things to eat.

THE TRAIL TO GOLD. Take one part of the story and make a play. The part where the Indian boy wants to trade his bow and arrow for Ellen's cat would make a good play.

THE TINDER BOX. In pantomime, have the dog carry the princess to the soldier. Have the lady-in-waiting follow the dog and make a mark on the gate. What other parts of the story would be fun to pantomime?

GEORGIE. Pretend you are a quiet ghost in your own living room. Tell the class what you would see there. How do you think a ghost would walk?

UNIT FIVE

HOLIDAYS ARE FUN

RIDDLE:

WHAT
AM I?

Dorothy Aldis

They chose me from my brothers: "That's the
Nicest one," they said,
And they carved me out a face and put a
Candle in my head;

And they set me on the doorstep.   Oh, the
Night was dark and wild;
But when they lit the candle, then I
Smiled!

From *Hop, Skip and Jump* by Dorothy Aldis. Copyright, 1934, by G. P. Putnam's Sons.

GEORGIE

Robert Bright

In a little village in New England there was a little house which belonged to Mr. and Mrs. Whittaker.

Up in the little attic of this little house there lived a little ghost. His name was Georgie.

Every night at the same time he gave the loose board on the stairs a little creak and the parlor door a little squeak. And then Mr. and Mrs. Whittaker knew it was time to go to bed. And Herman, the cat, he knew it was time to prowl.

And as for Miss Oliver, the owl, she knew it was time to wake up and say "Whoo-oo-oo!"

And so it went, with everything as it should be, until Mr. Whittaker took it into his head to hammer a nail into the loose board on the stairs

and to oil the hinges of the parlor door. And so the stairs wouldn't creak any more and the door wouldn't squeak any more. And Mr. and Mrs. Whittaker didn't know when it was time to go to bed any more. And Herman — he didn't know when it was time to begin to prowl any more. And as for Miss Oliver, she didn't know when to wake up any more and went on sleeping.

And Georgie sat up in the attic and moped.

That was a fine how-do-you-do!

Pretty soon, though, Georgie decided to find some other house to haunt. But while he ran to this house and then to that house each house already had a ghost.

The only house in the whole village which didn't have a ghost was Mr. Gloams' place.

But that was so awfully gloomy! The big door *groaned* so! And the big stairway *moaned* so!

And besides, Mr. Gloams himself was such a crotchety old man, he came near frightening Georgie half to death.

So Georgie ran away to a cow barn where there lived a harmless cow.

But the cow paid no attention to Georgie. She just chewed her cud all the time, and it wasn't much fun.

Meanwhile, a lot of time went by and it rained a good deal and during the winter it snowed to

194

beat the band. And out at the cow barn Georgie was terribly cold and uncomfortable.

But what with the dampness from the rain and the coldness from the snow, something happened to that board on the Whittaker stairs and to the hinges on the Whittaker parlor door.

It was Herman who discovered it and told Miss Oliver. And she woke up with a start.

Miss Oliver flew right over to the cow barn to tell Georgie that the board on the stairs was loose again, and that the hinges on the parlor door were rusty again.

195

What glad tidings that was for Georgie! He ran right home lickety-split.

And so, at the same old time, the stairs creaked again and the parlor door squeaked again. And Mr. and Mrs. Whittaker knew when it was time to go to sleep again. And Herman, he knew when to begin to prowl again.

And as for Miss Oliver, she knew when it was time to wake up again and say "Whoo-oo-oo!"

Thank goodness!

WHAT HAPPENED?

Georgie wasn't a very big ghost. He only gave stairs *little* creaks. He only gave doors *little* squeaks. He didn't like Mr. Gloams' house. Why didn't he like Mr. Gloams' house? Where did Georgie live during the winter?

Finally Georgie came back to his old home. Everyone was glad. Why were they all glad?

THINK IT OVER

Ghosts are just pretend. But they scare some people anyway. Georgie didn't scare anybody. In fact, just the opposite happened at Mr. Gloams' house. Mr. Gloams scared Georgie! You didn't expect that, did you? That's one way to make a story funny. What is that way?

196

MR. GOAT'S THANKSGIVING

Miriam Clark Potter

Mr. Goat thought to himself that he would like to have a fine Thanksgiving dinner. He had noticed, every year before this, how very happy people were on that day; how they sat around at long tables and laughed and ate food.

So he went to market. He bought a big turkey, plenty of potatoes, onions, and squash; a lot of bread and butter, some elegant red jelly, and a fine big mince pie as large as a moon. He planned to eat and eat and eat, for the very next day was Thanksgiving.

That afternoon he went right to work cooking his things. He built up a big red fire in the stove; he put on a long blue and yellow apron with black spots on it. Under the bottom of his apron his queer black feet stuck out. He smiled, as he

smelled the good things; he frosted some chocolate cakes and stuffed the turkey.

Then he went to bed and slept. He looked funny in bed, with a green nightcap on over his horns.

The next day Mr. Goat began early, setting the table with a clean cloth, putting the little yellow jug of flowers on it, getting the food ready on plates, and roasting the turkey. "Soon I shall be laughing and eating happily, like all the people along the street," he said to himself.

Then the turkey was done, and he put it on the platter. He made the good brown gravy. He mashed the potatoes and set a lump of butter on them; it melted in the middle in a wee yellow

puddle. He creamed the onions, fixed the squash with pepper and salt, turned the elegant red jelly onto a dish, where it shook and shivered deliciously. At last everything was on the table, all ready for Mr. Goat. Even his tall glass was filled and the butter rolled up into round little balls.

Mr. Goat sat down. "It looks good," he said, as he sharpened his knife, "but I do not feel in the least like laughing happily, the way I hear people in the houses along the street doing. I wonder why?"

He decided to ask the mother cat, who lived next door with her four hungry yellow kittens. So he threw open the window and called her over, for she was airing her babies in the yard.

199

"I have prepared a fine dinner for Thanksgiving," he said, "just the way I have watched others do. They sit at the table and laugh and eat, and act very happy. I have the dinner, but I do not feel very happy. I do not feel like laughing. Why is it?"

Mrs. Cat thought. She wrinkled her face and shut her eyes. She looked very sleepy, thinking. Then all at once she opened her eyes wide and said, "I do not know, unless it is because you have no company to laugh with."

"That may be it!" Mr. Goat thought it was a good idea. "All the others have company — a whole crowd of it! Mrs. Cat, will you bring your babies over, and eat with me?"

Mrs. Cat smiled a gray maltese smile. She was very pleased. "I did not think of that," she told him, "but you are very kind, Mr. Goat. We will come."

200

So they came. She tied pink bibs around the necks of the kittens, and they climbed up into their chairs. Their tails stuck out behind. Mr. Goat set out a saucer of milk for each cat, because he knew they would like that, and their pink tongues lapped it up fast.

Then he said, "This is better. I am happier, but I still do not feel like laughing. Listen to those people across the street. How glad they sound! Why do you suppose it is, Mrs. Cat?"

Mrs. Cat thought again. She shut her eyes, and moved her whiskers. Then she said, "I don't know, unless it is because they are thankful."

"What is that?" asked Mr. Goat.

"They are glad that they have plenty of food and a nice place to eat it in, and good friends to visit with them," said Mrs. Cat. "So thankful that they are not all alone in a dark, cold place, with nothing at all!"

201

"Well, I am glad for that, too," Mr. Goat told her. "Things are very fortunate for me, and I want you and your kittens to have a nice good time here at my house. Now, come. Let me fill your plates with turkey and stuffing, and all these other things!"

The cat family passed their plates again and again. And they all laughed, Mr. Goat loudest of all. He was having a fine Thanksgiving dinner at last, for he had good food, company to eat it with, and a thankful feeling in his heart.

WHAT HAPPENED?

Mr. Goat cooked a wonderful Thanksgiving dinner. He wanted to be happy on Thanksgiving Day. But when he sat down to eat he didn't feel very happy. He didn't know why. But Mrs. Cat knew. What did Mrs. Cat tell Mr. Goat?

Mr. Goat decided to do what Mrs. Cat said. What did he do? Was Mrs. Cat right?

THINK IT OVER

Not every family is happy at Thanksgiving time. A good dinner doesn't always make people happy. Mr. Goat found that out. You can help your family to be happy at Thanksgiving. What can you do to help?

202

THE SNOWMAN

Frances Frost

We made a snowman in our yard,
Jolly, and round, and fat.
We gave him Father's pipe to smoke
And Father's battered hat.
We tied a red scarf around his neck,
And in his buttonhole
We stuck a holly spray.
He had black buttons made of coal.
He had black eyes, a turned up nose,
A wide and cheerful grin;
And there he stood in our front yard,
Inviting company in!

CHRISTMAS

Marchette Chute

My goodness, my goodness,
It's Christmas again.
The bells are all ringing.
I do not know when
I've been so excited.
The tree is all fixed,
The candles are lighted,
The pudding is mixed.
The wreath's on the door
And the carols are sung,
The presents are wrapped
And the holly is hung.
The turkey is sitting
All safe in its pan,
And I am behaving
As calm as I can.

Reprinted by permission of the author.

JOURNEY
FOR A CHRISTMAS STAR
Richard E. Drdek

Tommy was the first one to see the rocket ship on the back lawn. He had been looking out the window, watching the sky for a sign of reindeer and sleigh, when his gaze drifted down to the yard. There, resting on a thin layer of snow in the moonlight, was a rocket ship. He yelled the news to Timmy. Before long, the boys, still in pajamas, were running down the steps, across the snow, and into the ship.

"Let's try it," said Tommy. "Let's take a trip."

"All right. Let's," Timmy said. "Where shall we go?"

Tommy thought for a long time. Then he said, "It's Christmas Eve, and our first trip should mean something. Maybe we could try to find the lost Christmas Star."

Used by permission of the author.

Timmy liked the idea very much. He knew the story about the bright shiny star that had led the Three Wise Men to Bethlehem. And he knew that the star had never been seen after that one time.

"Where could we look for it?" he asked.

"We'll start with the Big Dipper," said Tommy. "We'll go all over the sky if we have to."

They strapped themselves into their seats and zoomed into the sky. The rocket ship headed straight for the Big Dipper. When they got there, the boys weren't a bit surprised to see it filled with water. Pilot Tommy circled the cup of the Dipper intending to make a seaplane landing. But instead of water they landed on ice. They slid and skidded and spun around and around.

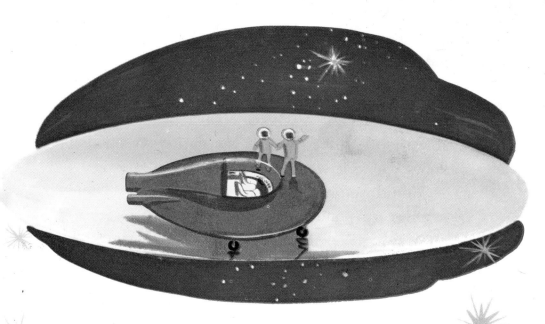

"Look!" Tommy said. "It's ice!"

A deep, booming voice roared out of the darkness. "What did you expect to find, lemon pie?"

"Who — who are you?" asked Tommy in a shaky voice.

"I'm the Dipper Tender," the voice roared. "What — are — you — doing — on — my — skating — pond?"

The two boys could see no one. It was coal black dark. The booming voice coming out of nowhere was almost too much for them. But they tried to be as brave as they could.

"We're Tommy and Timmy, the Watson twins," they said. "We came here looking for the Christmas Star. Can you please help us?"

The big gruff voice suddenly became soft and friendly. "The Christmas Star? I wish I knew where to find it. It was such a beautiful thing. It was so bright it lighted the entire sky. I don't know where it went, but I wish I did know."

"Could you tell us who might know?" Timmy asked very politely.

"Maybe Leo the Lion could tell you," the Dipper Tender said. "Go see him. He's always looking at the sky. He may have seen something."

Tommy and Timmy thanked him and took off again. This time they landed right next to Leo. The big lion stood there, looking across the sky. Even when the boys landed next to him, he kept his eyes fixed in space.

"I beg your pardon," Tommy said, "but have you seen the Christmas Star?"

Without turning his head or taking his eyes off the skies, Leo answered, "For two thousand years I've been watching and waiting. For two thousand years I've wanted to be the first to see the Christmas Star, if it should ever appear again. It has never come back."

"Do you have any idea where the Star has gone?" Timmy asked.

"All I know," Leo said sadly, "is that the Star

has gone from the skies. I've heard it said that it still lives. That's why I'm waiting for it to come back. But I don't know where it has gone."

"Do you know anyone who might know?" asked Tommy.

"Go to the Milky Way and talk to the Herdsman," Leo said. "If anyone knows where the Star has gone, he does. He sees many things and he knows many things. He is the wise man of the sky."

The two boys thanked the lion and were off again. They flew toward that huge splash of stars which looked as if someone had splattered whipped cream across the sky. Timmy thought it looked good enough to eat. He wanted Tommy to fly close so that he could reach out and skim some of it off, like scooping up cake icing.

"That isn't real milk," Tommy laughed.

"I know," said Timmy, "but it's nice to pretend."

They landed in the middle of the Milky Way and started to look for the Herdsman. He was off to one side of his flock, herding several young wandering stars back into the fold. When he saw the boys, he came hurrying toward them.

The Herdsman of the Milky Way was a tall

man with a long white beard — so long that he almost stepped on the end of it.

"Bless me, bless me," the Herdsman said. "What have we here? Did you boys come to hear a bedtime story?"

"No, sir," said Tommy. "We came to ask you about the Christmas Star."

The Herdsman ran his hand down his beard and gave it a tug. "Ah, the Christmas Star! What do you want to know about it?"

"We're looking for it," said Timmy. "Can you tell us where it is?"

The Herdsman tugged at his beard again and said, "If I can get into that flying machine of yours, I'll show you where it is."

After the three of them squeezed into the rocket ship, the Herdsman pointed to the earth and said, "Fly down there."

Tommy gave the ship full blast power and away they roared. When they arrived over Earth, the Herdsman pointed to a large building with a steeple. The building was bright with light.

"What is that?" he asked.

"A church," said Timmy. "It's a church full of people. They're singing songs about Christmas."

They landed and the Herdsman took them to a house. He told the boys to look in the window and tell him what they saw.

"I see a mother and father and three children sitting by a fire," Tommy said. "Stockings are hanging by the fireplace. The father is telling Christmas stories."

They went to another house, a poorer house. They looked in a window and the Herdsman said, "Tell me what you see."

"A little boy and a girl are putting pieces of colored paper on a Christmas tree," Timmy answered. "They're laughing and having a lot of fun."

The Herdsman took the two boys back to the rocket ship. "Now do you know where the Christmas Star is? Did you see it?"

Both boys nodded.

The Herdsman continued, "The Christmas Star shines in those people who keep Christmas. Those people in church singing Christmas songs are keeping the Star alive. The Star shines in the home of the mother and father telling Christmas stories to their children. You saw the little boy and girl fixing the tree. They are keeping Christmas. That's where the Star is. It shines

212

in the hearts of thousands of people who make Christmas what it is."

"Gee," said Tommy and Timmy.

"Now take me back to my Milky Way. Some of my young scampering stars might wander too far away."

Tommy and Timmy flew the Herdsman back to his flock. Before long they were in their beds again.

"Gee," said Timmy. "I'm sure glad we found the Star. Do you think we should keep it a secret, or should we tell people?"

"It's really not much of a secret," Tommy replied. "Those who keep Christmas know where it is. Those who don't keep it won't care to know."

Then the two very tired explorers went to sleep.

WHAT HAPPENED?

Tommy and Timmy zoomed into the sky. They went to the Big Dipper. They went to see Leo the Lion. Where else did they go?

The Herdsman knew where the Christmas Star was. Where did they find it? What was the Christmas Star?

THINK IT OVER

This is a pretend story. How do you know it is pretend?

Everybody likes holidays. Christmas is one holiday which many people celebrate. Hanukkah is another holiday when many people give presents. What do you like about Christmas or Hanukkah?

Tommy and Timmy found that a big part of Christmas is making other people happy. What do you do at Christmas or at Hanukkah to make people happy?

It is fun to get presents. It is also fun to give presents. What fun do you have when you give somebody a present?

THE RUNAWAY VALENTINE

Doris Litterly

In the top row of valentines at Dawson's Card Shop there was a fat little red heart. He had arms and legs and a painted face. The words BE MY VALENTINE were printed on his other side, and the little valentine thought his name was BEMY VALENTINE.

Bemy didn't have any flowers or lace or ribbons on him, like the other valentines. He thought they were all sissies.

"This is no place for me," he said. "I'm going out and see the rest of the world." So he jumped down from the stand and walked out the door of the shop.

The very minute Bemy stepped outside, a man tramped on him. It wasn't the man's fault. No

Reprinted by permission of *Highlights for Children Magazine*.

215

one expects valentines to be walking around on the sidewalk.

"Oh, well," Bemy said, brushing himself off, "now I really look tough." He limped across the walk, watching carefully for people.

Because he was watching for people and not looking where he was going, he stepped right off the sidewalk into the gutter. The water carried him down, down, down. At last the water slowed down a little. He climbed back onto the street.

The water had washed off most of Bemy's red paint. He looked very wet. And he sneezed several times.

"Aw," he said, "tough guys like me don't catch cold." So he started on across the street.

HONK! He jumped straight up in the air as a huge truck zoomed by him. HONK! A car passed him from the other direction. Bemy hopped across the street.

"Whew," he said, "that was terrible." He sat down to rest for a minute.

A great black dog came running up to him. It sniffed at Bemy, licked him once. Then it went on its way.

"Out of my way," screamed a little boy on roller skates. Bemy wasn't quite fast enough. One of the wheels ran right over his legs, bending them so he couldn't walk straight.

"Oh," thought the little valentine, "this is awful. Maybe I'm not so tough as I thought."

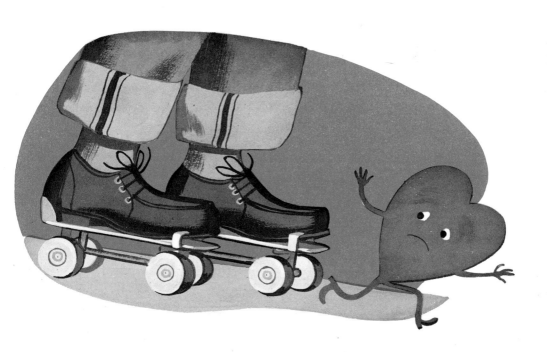

He looked sadly at the card shop across the street. Then he looked at all the cars. He could never make it back to the shop.

Bemy sat down on the sidewalk with his little pointed chin in his hands. He sniffed. He wasn't too tough to catch a cold, after all. A big tear formed in each eye and rolled down his cheeks. It washed away the last of the red paint. He saw himself in the gutter water below him. He was certainly a sad-looking valentine. No one would buy him, even if he could get back to the card shop. Another tear rolled down his cheek.

"Look, Mary, it's a valentine."

Bemy was frightened when he saw the boy coming toward him. But the boy picked him up gently.

"It must have got lost," the girl said softly. Bemy nodded his head. Of course the boy and girl thought it was just the wind making him move.

"Do you want it?" the boy asked.

"Oh, yes. I think it's cute." The girl reached for Bemy. She straightened his crooked little legs. "I'll take it home and paste it in my album."

Bemy sank down in the warm darkness inside the girl's purse. These were very nice children. He didn't know what an album was, but he was

sure it would be nice, too. And it would be very nice to have a home again.

WHAT HAPPENED?

Bemy wanted to run away. He wanted to see the world. So he went away from the card shop. What happened to him first after he left the shop? What happened next? What happened when the boy on skates came along?

Bemy decided he should go back home. He felt sad. Why didn't he go back to the card shop? Where did Bemy finally go? Can you make up a story about his life there?

THINK IT OVER

Bemy wanted to see the world. He thought it would be more exciting than his home. He finally decided that home was a pretty good place to be, after all. Have you ever felt like Bemy did? What are some of the good things about your home? Why do you think it is the best place in the world?

Bemy was homesick after he left the card shop. Have you ever been homesick? That is not a happy feeling. Tell the class about some time when you were homesick. What happened to make you feel better?

LONG AGO
AND FAR AWAY

THE TRAIL

TO GOLD

Clyde Robert Bulla

Many years ago Frank and Ellen and their family set out for California. They traveled in wagons with some other families. Ellen had her kitten named Nugget with her.

The wagons rolled across Kansas. Before many days Frank and Ellen knew everyone in the wagon train.

They knew the scouts, Buck and Tony. Sometimes the scouts rode ahead to watch for Indians.

They knew Bill Miller, the boy from Illinois. He was older than they were, but he liked to play with them. At night they played hide-and-seek among the wagons, or they sat by the campfire and talked.

Ellen liked the nights best of all. The wagons were pulled up in a circle. The animals were tied where they could eat grass. The men built fires.

After supper everyone sat around the campfires. Some of the men told stories and sang songs. One man played his fiddle. Frank and Ellen wanted him to play on and on. But after a while someone would say, "Time for bed. We have to get up early in the morning."

Frank liked the nights, but he liked the days better. Every day there were new things to see. There were wolves on the prairie. There were buffalo herds.

Sometimes Buck, one of the scouts, took him for a horseback ride.

One day Buck said, "I'm going ahead to look for water. Do you want to ride with me?"

Frank climbed up behind him. They rode away.

"See those trees?" said Buck. "We may find water there."

They rode across the prairie. They stopped under the trees.

Among the trees Frank saw a high, rocky bank. Water ran out of it and into a pool below.

"It's a big spring," said Frank.

"See those tracks around the pool?" said Buck. "Wild animals come here to drink. This is their water hole."

"There is one that looks like a man's track," said Frank.

"It *is* a man's track!" said Buck.

Just then the horse jumped.

"Look!" cried Frank.

High on the bank above the pool stood an Indian. He wore only a few clothes. His face was painted green.

For a moment he stood there. Then he was gone behind the rocks.

"Hold on, Frank!" said Buck. He turned the horse around. They rode back to the wagon as fast as they could go.

"We saw an Indian," said Buck.

People called from wagon to wagon, "An Indian! They saw an Indian!"

Jim Welles told the men to drive the wagons up in a circle. "Everyone stay inside the circle," he said. "Keep the animals inside, too. These Indians may be friendly, but load your guns and be ready."

Mr. Davis helped get the guns ready. Mrs. Davis, Frank, and Ellen got into the wagon. Frank looked out the back.

Far out on the prairie he saw something move. It was a man on a horse. Behind him came more men on horses.

Frank tried to count them. He told Ellen,

"There must be fifty Indians."

Ellen looked out. "I see some with their faces painted green."

"They look like the one I saw by the water hole," said Frank. "See the man in front, on the spotted pony? He must be the chief."

"They don't have guns," said Ellen.

"No," said Frank, "but they have bows and arrows."

Close to the wagons the Indians stopped. The Indian in front held up his hand.

"Friend!" he said.

The other Indians said it, too. "Friend — friend!"

The men came out from behind the wagons. The Indians made signs to show that they wanted

226

to trade with the white men. They had furs and horses to trade.

"No," said Jim Welles. "We have horses, and we don't need furs. But we are glad you are our friends. Will you eat with us?"

The Indians got off their horses and sat on the ground.

The women and some of the men built a fire and made coffee. They brought out ham and corncakes.

"Good, good!" said the Indians. They ate with both hands. They burned their mouths on the hot coffee.

Frank and Ellen stood near them. Ellen had Nugget in her arms.

227

An Indian boy came up to her. He patted the kitten's head. "Mew-cat," he said. He pointed to the kitten, then to his bow and arrow.

"He wants to trade his bow and arrow for your cat," said her father.

"Oh, no!" She ran away and hid Nugget in the wagon. Frank ran with her. He took his old knife out of the wagon and went back to the Indian boy.

"Will you trade your bow and arrow for this?" he asked.

The Indian boy held out his hand. He took the knife and gave Frank the bow and arrow.

When the Indians had eaten all the food, they went to their horses. As they rode away, the Indian boy looked back.

"Good-by," he said, and waved the knife.

"Good-by," said Frank, and waved the bow and arrow.

Ellen looked out of the wagon. She had Nugget in her arms. The Indian boy saw them.

"Good-by, mew-cat!" he said.

It sounded so funny that Frank and Ellen began to laugh. But the Indian boy looked sad.

Indians came out nearly every day to see the wagon train. They were friendly, and they all wanted to eat.

228

"If we feed them all," said Mrs. Davis, "we won't have enough food for ourselves."

But they always had food on the prairie. They had buffalo meat, and they caught fish. Once they found some wild strawberries, red and ripe and sweet.

They came to the end of the prairie. There were rivers to cross. When the water was not deep, they could drive through it. When it was deep, the men had to make a ferry-boat to take the wagons across.

Summer came, and the trail grew dry and dusty. The dust made Frank and Ellen sneeze.

Sometimes the air was full of bugs. They were big, brown bugs. They flew into the wagon. The cat patted them with his paws.

"Let's go fast," said Ellen, "and get away from the bugs."

"There are worse things than bugs," her mother told her.

Ellen found out that there *were* worse things than bugs. There were long, hot days. There were mountains to cross.

Some of the wagons were too heavy. The animals could not pull them up the mountains.

"Lighten the load!" said Jim Welles.

Up and down the wagon train, people called to

229

each other, "Lighten the load — lighten the load!"

They threw out everything they could do without. They threw out horseshoes and boxes and tables and chairs.

At last the animals could pull the wagons up the trail.

There was a desert to cross. There was no water on the desert. For days the wagons rolled through dust and sand.

"The sun is so hot," said Ellen. "I wish I had a drink of water."

"So do I," said Frank.

"I wish we had more water," said their father, "but the animals have to drink and we have to drink. Now the water is nearly gone."

One day Frank was riding in front with his father. Ellen and her mother and Nugget were in back of the wagon.

"Look at Spud and Spike," said Frank. "See how their ears hang down."

"The mules are tired," said his father. "They want water, too."

All at once the mules lifted their heads. Their ears stood up. They began to go faster.

"Do you know what I think?" said Mr. Davis. "I think Spud and Spike smell water."

"Can mules smell water?" asked Frank.

"Yes, and horses can, too. Sometimes they can smell water for miles."

They moved along. Ellen went to sleep in the back of the wagon. It was evening when Frank shouted, "Ellen, wake up!"

In the wagons ahead, people were shouting, "Water — water!"

Ellen sat up and looked out. There were trees ahead. There was green grass. And there was a river.

People jumped out of their wagons. They ran to the river. They dipped water up in their hands and drank it.

231

"Isn't it cool! Isn't it good!" they cried.

Frank and Ellen lay down by the water and drank. Spud and Spike drank. All the other animals drank.

They stayed by the river that night. They made big campfires. The fiddler got out his fiddle and played. But the best music of all was the sound of the river.

For three days they camped there. The women washed clothes and cooked. The men cut trees and made a big raft out of logs. They took the animals and wagons across the river on the raft.

After that there were more rivers. There were mountains, too.

One night the wagon train stopped on the side of a mountain. Frank and Ellen sat by their campfire.

"We've been on the road a long time," said Ellen.

"Yes," said Frank. "It was spring when we started. Now it will soon be fall."

"Nugget was a kitten when we started," said Ellen. "Now he is a big cat."

A man came out of the trees and sat down.

"Hello," he said. "Where are you from?"

"Missouri," said Frank.

"Do you live on this mountain?" asked Ellen.

"No," said the man. "I came here to find gold."

"Is there gold here?" asked Frank.

"There is gold all around us," said the man. "This is California, and the gold fields are just ahead."

In the morning Frank and his father went out to look for gold. Frank took a pan. His father took a pick and shovel.

Men were digging by the river.

"Is it all right if we dig here, too?" asked Mr. Davis.

"Yes," said one of the men, "if you can find a place."

They found a place where no one was working. Frank dug up some dirt with the pick. His father took it up in the shovel and put it into the pan.

He sat on a rock by the river. Frank stood close to him while he filled the pan with water.

Mr. Davis stirred the dirt until it was soft. He held the pan under the water and the mud washed away.

233

"Now only rocks are left," he said. "If there is gold, it will be under the rocks, in the bottom of the pan."

"Why?" asked Frank.

"Because the gold is so heavy," his father told him. "It is heavier than the sand or rocks."

"Do you think there is gold in this pan?" asked Frank.

"We'll soon find out." Mr. Davis took out the rocks and threw them away. He looked in the bottom of the pan. "Nothing there," he said.

They tried another pan, and another. All the morning they worked, but they found no gold.

They went back to the tent city. Mrs. Davis and Ellen had dinner ready.

"Have you found gold?" asked Ellen.

"Not yet," said Frank.

"I hope you find some today," said Mrs. Davis. "Things cost so much at the store, we need gold to pay for them."

"I know how to pan gold now," said Frank. "I wish I had a pan."

"Could you use my wooden bowl?" asked his mother.

"I can try it," said Frank.

When he and his father went back to the river, Frank took the wooden bowl. At first they worked together. Then Frank went a little way up the river.

A man called to him, "Are you finding any gold?"

"No," said Frank.

"Look for a place where the dirt is blue," the man told him. "Blue dirt is the best for gold."

Frank found a place where the dirt was blue. He filled the bowl with dirt. He dipped the bowl into the river and washed out all the mud. One

235

by one he picked out the rocks. In the bottom of the bowl were a few little specks. They were yellow.

He ran to his father, "I think I've found gold!"

His father looked at the yellow specks. "I think you have, too. Go to the store and show them to the man who buys gold. Ask him if this is really gold."

Frank ran to the tent city. He saw his mother and Ellen in front of the tent.

"Where are you going?" asked Ellen.

"I think I have some gold," said Frank. "I'm going to the store to find out."

"I want to go, too," said Ellen. "Please?"

"Run along, then," said Mrs. Davis.

"Come on, Ellen," said Frank. They ran through the town. People shouted at them as they went by, "Is that bowl full of gold?" Two boys and a dog began to run behind them.

Frank and Ellen ran into the store.

A man came up to them. "What can I do for you?"

Frank held out the bowl. "Will you tell me if this is gold?"

The man looked at the yellow specks. He rubbed them between his fingers. "It's gold," he said.

"Thank you," said Frank. He took Ellen's hand. "Let's go back and tell Father!"

WHAT HAPPENED?

When the wagon train stopped at night, Frank and Ellen played with the other children. What did they play?

One day some Indians came to the wagon camp. What did the Indian boy want to trade for with Ellen? What did he trade for with Frank?

The wagon train needed water. What did the people do when they came at last to a river?

Finally the wagons came to California. Who found the first gold? How did he know that it was real gold?

THINK IT OVER

Every night on the trip the wagons were put into a circle. Can you think of a good reason why they were put into a circle?

Ellen and Frank were taking a trip. How was their trip different from a trip you might take?

237

JOHNNY AM A LINGO LAY

Clyde Bulla

238

From *The Secret Valley*. Copyright, 1949, by Clyde Robert Bulla. Reprinted by permission of the publisher, Thomas Y. Crowell Company.

STEVIE'S FLUTE

Helen Boyd Higgins

This story tells about Stephen Foster when he was a boy. He lived a long time ago before the days of automobiles or paved streets. Part of our country was not even settled then. Stephen Foster grew up to be one of America's greatest song writers. Two of his songs are "My Old Kentucky Home" and "Jeannie."

When Stevie was seven he and Ma and Pa were visiting in Pittsburgh. They were staying with friends whom they had known when they lived in the White Cottage.

Today they had come downtown in a hired hack. Pa had some business to attend to. Ma was going to do some shopping. Stevie was going to look around. He liked that.

"Now," said Pa, "I'll leave you two here. I'll come for you in three hours. Will that be time enough for you, my dear?"

From *Stephen Foster: Boy Minstrel* by Helen Boyd Higgins, copyright, 1944. Used by special permission of the publishers, The Bobbs-Merrill Company, Inc.

Ma smiled. She stepped carefully from the hack to the high walk. The streets were very muddy in Pittsburgh. Stevie jumped down after her. Pa waved to them and was soon gone.

"Stevie," said Ma, "I'm going into this store. You may go anywhere you like as long as you stay on this street."

Stevie nodded. Ma disappeared through the store door. Stevie was by himself. He looked about to see what to do first.

There, right across the street, was a great covered wagon, a Conestoga wagon. Four brown oxen were hitched to it. A man with a red beard rode on a white horse beside them. Stevie knew now what he wanted to do.

He picked his way through the mud that almost covered his high-buttoned shoes; he had always wanted to see inside a covered wagon.

Stevie saw a boy lean forward from the front seat of the wagon.

242

"You stay here, Bud," said the man on the horse. "We'll bring you some bullets for your gun. Keep your eye on everything."

The boy grinned and pulled off his wide-brimmed hat. He wiped his hot face on his sleeve. A tall woman and a little girl climbed out of the back of the wagon. Everyone left but "Bud."

Stevie stood near the big front wheel. "Hello," he said.

"Hello," said the big boy. "Hello, Bud."

"My name isn't Bud," said Stevie. "I thought that was your name."

"My name's David," said the boy. "Jake just calls me Bud. What's your name?"

"Stephen Foster."

The two boys looked at each other.

"Want to come up and sit a spell while Pop's gone?" said David. "I got a new gun I can show you."

Stevie climbed up on the axle of the great wooden wheel.

"Here, I'll give you a hand," said David. "You ain't much bigger than Effie."

"Who's Effie?" asked Stevie.

"My sister. She just went off with Mom."

"Oh," said Stevie.

Then neither spoke. David was looking at the gun which lay across his knees. Stevie waited. David began to rub the barrel of the gun with some rags.

"Where you going?" finally Stevie asked.

"Indiany," said David.

"Is that far?" asked Stevie.

"Yep."

"Can you shoot?" asked Stevie.

"Sure," said David.

Stevie began to look about him. It was almost dark inside the wagon, but he could see the out-line of furniture, barrels, boxes, and some clothes hanging up on the braces of the canvas cover. It was lighter toward the back.

Stevie started to climb into the wagon.

"Where you goin'?" said David. "Pop wouldn't want strangers in there."

"I want to see that banjo that's hanging up on the door. Is it yours?"

"Nope, that's Jake's."

"Who's Jake?" asked Stevie.

"Say, you're a great one for asking questions, ain't you?" said David.

Stevie waited. He wondered if David would answer his last question.

"Jake's the man that's ridin' with us. He sure can make that banjo play," said David.

"What does he play? What kind of tunes, I mean."

"Lots of tunes. He plays when we settle down for the night. It's mighty comfortin' then," said David.

"Comforting?" said Stevie.

"Don't you know nothing?" said David. "Comfortin' makes you feel safer like when it's lonesome."

Stevie understood. He was sorry he had asked. He changed the subject. "Is it fun riding to Indiany?"

"Sometimes. It's mighty cold nights. There might be Indians out west. Jake says there's some in Indiany."

Stevie turned to look at the oxen. He wished Jake would come. Maybe he would play a tune for him. "Do you ride all night?" he asked.

"No," said David.

"What if Indians are around? What do you do then?"

"Shoot 'em before they shoots us."

For a minute Stevie was quiet. He looked again back into the wagon.

"I wish Jake would play his banjo when he comes. Will he?"

"Maybe. Jake's the best player in these parts. He takes all the prizes. You can't keep your feet still when Jake plays."

"Here comes your father," said Stevie suddenly. "Is that Jake?"

"Sure. Sure. That's Jake and my uncle and Pop and Mom and Effie. I guess we'll be goin' now."

"Can I ask Jake to play?" asked Stevie.

David didn't answer. He had jumped down and was helping lift a large box into the back of the wagon. Stevie heard him say, "That boy up in front is Stephen, Pop. He wanted to see Jake's banjo. I didn't let him."

244

Stevie's face flushed. He started to get down. No one was paying attention to him. He turned and was ready to climb over the wheel when he heard a new voice. "Do you play the banjo, Son?"

"No, sir," said Stevie.

The man who was standing by him was very tall. His eyes were blue. He smiled broadly.

"Want to hear Mamie play, do you?" he asked.

"Mamie?" said Stevie.

"My banjo. All good banjos has names, Son. Jest like people. Mamie's the best little gal in these parts."

"Will you — make her sing?" said Stevie.

Jake threw back his head and laughed and laughed. "Bust my strings I will," he said. "Come on, young'un. I'll learn you how Mamie kin sing."

Jake took the banjo from its peg. He patted it and blew on the strings and wiped off the dust with his sleeve.

"What'll it be, Son?" he said.

245

Stevie shook his head. He was so excited he couldn't speak.

Jake began to play. People on the street stopped walking and came over to the wagon. David was right. No one could keep his feet still when Jake played.

He sang, too. It was a song which Stevie had never heard. It was a lively dancing song. Then, with another tune, Mamie was crying. Then he played "Hail Columbia" and everyone sang.

When Jake played, Stevie could almost feel how lonely it was out on the way to Indiana.

"Don't know how we'd make it without Mamie," said Jake. "She'll have to hang up now till night. We gotta be goin'. Here comes the missus."

It took a very short time for all David's family to climb into the great covered wagon.

Stevie hurried around to the front of the wagon to say good-by. But David was looking toward the West and Indiana.

"Good-by," Stevie shouted.

David didn't turn.

The wagon rumbled off down the street. Jake sprang onto his white horse. He rode by the side of the oxen. He carried a long whip which he circled over their backs.

"See you in Indiany!" he shouted back to Stevie.

Stevie waved. The wagon rounded the corner and was gone. The crowd was soon gone, too. Stevie crossed the street and began to look into the store windows.

"I wish I could make up a song like those Jake plays," he said to himself.

The sound of Jake's music was still ringing in Stevie's ear, when he heard another kind of music. It came from farther down the street.

"I wonder who's playing the piano on this street?" said Stevie to himself.

He hurried down the board walk and saw a crowd of men standing in the doorway of a small shop called the Smith and Mellon's Music Shop. The music was coming from just beyond the men. Stevie pushed his way under their arms. There he saw a strange sight, and he heard a salesman

say, "It's the first upright piano ever to be seen outside of Philadelphia. My friend John Isaac Hawkins invented it."

"Who's he?" asked one of the men.

"He's an Englishman who lives in Philadelphia. The pianos we've had before take up so much room when they're moved. This one can easily be sent in a Conestoga wagon or by barge on the river."

"It sounds just the same as a piano," said Stevie.

No one had noticed him before. He stood near the instrument.

"May I play it a little?" he asked.

"Certainly not," said the young salesman.

"It's very valuable. It belongs to Henry Kleber, the musician. He wouldn't want a child banging on it."

"But I wouldn't bang. I just want to see how —"

"No, run along now, Sonny. Where's your mother?" said another man.

"But I can play it. Please let me," said Stevie.

But the man pushed him away. Stevie looked about him as he walked toward the door. There were many musical instruments in cases. Among others was a banjo and a violin. Right on the

front counter was something which Stevie had never seen before.

It was small and black. It looked a little like Uncle Struthers' whistle. Stevie stopped and stood on tiptoe. No one was watching him now. They had all gone back to the upright piano.

Stevie took the small instrument into his hands and held it carefully. He lifted it to his mouth. There was a small hole near the end, just as there was on Uncle Struthers' whistle. Stevie blew into this. There was a sweet sound.

He pressed his fingers over the holes which were cut into the side. The sound changed. He blew softly again. It was a tune.

Stevie forgot that he was in a store and that the man who had tried to put him out would probably do so again. He played a little louder. He began to play one of his favorite tunes. It was "Hail Columbia."

"Here, here! What are you doing back in this store?" said the young storekeeper. "Go along. Put that flageolet down."

"Don't bother the lad, Burnes," said a new voice. "He is remarkable."

"But Mr. Kleber, that is our best —"

"Shaw! Let the boy alone."

Stevie heard them talking. He was glad that the taller of the two men was the boss. He played on and on. The men gathered about him. Stevie liked this. He liked to have people listen to him.

Then he heard his mother's voice.

"Stevie," she said. "Stevie, you must come now."

"But Madam," said his new friend, "your boy is truly remarkable. He must take many lessons. I myself will teach him."

"I'm afraid not," said Mother Foster. "His father has other plans for him. Come, Stevie."

"Oh, Ma," said Stevie. "May I have this? May I, Ma?"

"Of course he must have the flageolet, Madam," said the older musician. "He is gifted beyond anyone of his age whom I have ever heard."

Mother Foster was very pleased. She thought quickly. The Fosters had very little money. She

250

decided that she really could wear her old, old
dress again so that she might buy the little flute
for Stevie.

When they left the store he carried the treasure
with him.

When they were joined by Mr. Foster, Stevie
showed him the flageolet. He began to play a
lively little tune for his father. His father was
very angry.

"I simply won't have it, my dear," he said.
"Music is not for boys. Put it away, Stevie."

Stevie was disappointed. He put the new gift
back into its box.

"Pa," he said, "Mr. Kleber, at the music store,

had a new kind of piano, too. It looks like a box. It stands up instead of lying down. It was made by a man in Philadelphia whose name is Mr. Hawkins. Maybe I could make a new kind of a piano someday."

"Now you see, my dear," said Pa. "He thinks of nothing but music. I doubt if he ever heard of Robert Fulton and his steamboat the *Clermont*. Did you, Stevie?"

Stevie shook his head.

"But William, the boy is only seven. He isn't very grown-up yet," said Ma.

"But he knows how to play the flute and he knows who has made the newest type of piano," said Mr. Foster.

Mother Foster didn't answer. The trip home to Harmony was a very quiet one. But Stevie didn't mind. He had his new flageolet.

WHAT HAPPENED?

Jake talked about his banjo as if it were a real person. What name did he have for his banjo?

Stevie was a good player himself. In the music store he found a small, black flute. What did the storekeeper call the flute?

Stevie's father thought music was not for boys. What did his mother think? How do you know?

THINK IT OVER

David was going all the way to Indiana. In covered wagon days it was lonesome at night on such a trip. What helped that lonesome feeling?

Maybe you can play a flute or a piano or something else. Maybe you like to sing. What would be a good song for a lonesome feeling?

OLD DOG TRAY

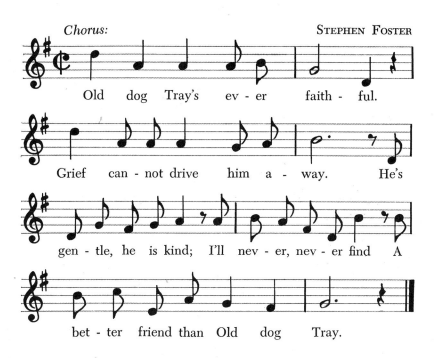

Chorus: STEPHEN FOSTER

Old dog Tray's ev - er faith - ful. Grief can - not drive him a - way. He's gen - tle, he is kind; I'll nev - er, nev - er find A bet - ter friend than Old dog Tray.

BIRTHDAY SURPRISES FOR MANUELA

Laura Bannon

Day after day Manuela thought of the beautiful American doll that she had seen in the city. Manuela lived in a small village in Mexico. One day her father had taken her to Mexico City. It was the first time she had been away from home.

There had been many wonderful things to see in the city, but Manuela remembered the American doll best of all. It was a little girl doll with blue eyes and yellow hair. Manuela had never seen blue eyes and yellow hair before. Her own eyes were black, and her hair was black. It stood out stiffly from her head in two short braids.

From *Manuela's Birthday* by Laura Bannon, illustrated by the author, and reprinted by permission of Albert Whitman & Company, publishers.

Most wonderful of all, this American doll wore a bonnet on her head. In all her life Manuela had never worn a bonnet or a hat. She didn't need a hat because she wrapped a long shawl about her head and shoulders. This shawl was called a *rebozo.*

Her mother wore a *rebozo* much larger than Manuela's. It was large enough to wrap around the baby brother when her mother carried him.

Manuela's father did not wear a *rebozo.* He had a large, fine hat. This hat was so large that he sometimes carried things in it as if it were a basket. . . .

Manuela wanted a little girl doll. She wanted a doll with blue eyes and yellow hair. That is why Manuela thought of the American doll day after day.

255

One day some Americans came to Manuela's village to paint pictures. While they painted a picture of Manuela's house, she talked to them and told them about her dolls. She also told them about her birthday.

"I shall be five years old tomorrow."

"And will you get more dolls on your birthday?" they asked.

"I hope so," said Manuela. "I would like a little girl doll with blue eyes and yellow hair, like the American doll in Mexico City."

That night Manuela dreamed of many dolls flying through the air. The prettiest doll of all had blue eyes and yellow hair.

The next morning the Americans got up early and went to every shop in the village. They were looking for a doll with blue eyes and yellow hair, but not a single American doll could they find.

Manuela's little Mexican friends had gotten up early, too. They were planning a surprise for her, and they had much to do.

First, they cut long strips of blue and yellow and red paper. Then they gathered large banana leaves and many flowers and carried them to the gate of Manuela's home. They were going to trim the gate in honor of her birthday. They wanted to surprise Manuela, so they worked oh, so quietly.

Inside the house, Manuela was just waking up. As soon as her eyes were wide open she remembered. "Today I am five years old! Now I may open the birthday package that came in the mail two days ago."

Manuela had felt of the package many times, trying to guess what was in it. She had decided that it was a little animal with long horns. Off came the paper wrapping and there were the horns, but no animal! It was a pair of green eyeglasses.

257

Manuela put them on and ran to the mirror. Could this be Manuela? But of course she looked different, for now she was five years old!

"There is a birthday present from your father and from me," said her mother. "You may have three guesses."

"I think it is candy or a sack of cookies."

"No, no."

"Could it be a little pig?"

"No, it is not a little pig. Why not go out in the yard and see for yourself, little one?"

Manuela ran outdoors and in the yard stood a baby burro — a very small, black, shaggy burro.

"Oh, thank you, Mother!" cried Manuela. "I must show him to Rosa and Tony and Pepito." And a happy little girl started toward the gate, leading the baby burro. . . .

Tony and Rosa and Pepito had made the loveliest kind of arch from the banana leaves and had decorated it with flowers and loops of colored paper. And right in the center, on one of the banana leaves, they had fastened five gay pink flowers to show that Manuela was five years old. It was the prettiest gate that Manuela had ever seen.

Even the baby burro stopped to look at it.

Soon the other boys and girls of the village came bringing bunches of flowers to Manuela. They had arranged them neatly against flat green leaves and tied them well. It was not long before all the jugs and pitchers and bowls that her mother could find were filled with flowers of many colors. . . .

All morning Manuela looked for the Americans

259

who had painted a picture of her home. She
wanted to show them her dear little baby burro.
She wondered if they had forgotten that this was
her birthday. Surely they would come to see her
today. This was the most special day of the whole
year for Manuela.

Over in the house where they were staying, the
American friends were as busy as they could be.
They found that they could not buy a little girl
doll like the one they wanted Manuela to have.
So they decided that they would make her an
American doll with blue eyes and yellow hair.

Going quickly from one shop to another, they
bought cloth and wool and ribbon. They had to
hunt a long time to get the color of yarn they
needed, but they found it at last. They bought
some baby sandals in the market. When they got
home they cut some buttons off their own clothes.

They placed all these things together and tried
to imagine the doll.

Then they began to work. From the white
cloth they cut the doll's body. They basted it
and stuffed it with wool just to see if it could
stand in its shoes. It stood very well. Then they
sewed it carefully. . . .

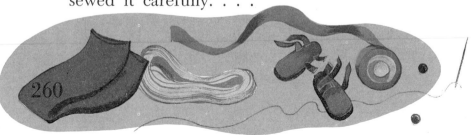

260

Next they made long hair out of yellow yarn which they had bought, and they sewed it on the doll's head. The yarn made very pretty hair. They hoped that Manuela would like it.

Now the doll was all ready for her clothes. The American friends saw that they must hurry, for it was getting late in the afternoon, and Manuela's birthday would soon be over. The clothes must be made quickly.

They gave the doll a haircut and braided her hair. They made a beautiful blue dress and put a pocket in it. They cut a handkerchief from grown-up size down to doll size. They made a blue bonnet to match the dress. They cut and sewed little socks and mittens.

When the doll was all dressed, the Americans thought she was very pretty. They put a flower in her bonnet and went to call on Manuela.

Manuela was playing in the back yard with her baby burro when her mother called, "Come and see what your American friends have brought you, little one."

Proudly wearing her new green birthday glasses, Manuela came running to her through a flock of chickens.

There on the table stood the American doll. She was looking right at Manuela. What a lovely doll she was, thought the little girl, with her beautiful dress, her bonnet, her mittens, and her shoes. Best of all, she had eyes that were a kind of blue.

Someone bumped against the table and the doll fell straight into Manuela's arms.

"Thank you very much," she said to the American friends. "The doll is very beautiful, and I really don't mind at all that her hair is green."

"For a little minute, Manuela, won't you take off your green glasses?" said her mother. "Even if you take them off, you will still be five years old."

So Manuela took off the green glasses. Then she saw that the doll really had yellow hair and blue eyes. Now everything was perfect. It was just the kind of doll that she had wanted for a long, long time.

She wrapped the doll in her *rebozo* just as her mother wrapped her baby brother. How happy she was! Manuela smiled up at her American

friends and they smiled down at her. She wanted to show this beautiful American doll to all her little friends.

Rosa and Tony and Pepito all wanted to hold the American doll. It was the most beautiful doll they had ever seen. They had never seen an American doll before, because they had never been to Mexico City.

"Today is really exciting," said Tony. "We must have a *recuerdo*."

"Let's ask the Americans to make a *recuerdo* for us," suggested Pepito.

So all four children went running back to Manuela's house. Manuela herself carried the doll, holding it close in her arms.

"What is a *recuerdo*?" asked the American friends, when Tony told them of the new birthday plan.

"It would be a picture painted to remember the day," the children explained. "We always like to have a *recuerdo* when something very special happens."

263

"We would like to have a picture of Manuela with the doll wrapped in her *rebozo*," said Rosa.

"The little baby burro must be in the picture, too," said Tony.

"A *recuerdo* is the very thing," agreed the American friends. "Wait right here, all of you, until we get our paints."

In a few minutes, the American friends were back with their paints. "Now, Manuela, get the burro," they said.

Then the American friends painted Manuela's fifth birthday *recuerdo*. And when it was finished, what a lovely one it was! There was Manuela in the picture, holding the beautiful doll with blue eyes and yellow hair.

The doll was wrapped in Manuela's *rebozo*, just as if it were a real baby. And there was the little baby burro in the picture, too.

264

"Almost I think you could speak out of that picture," said Manuela's mother. "It is beautiful."

Manuela's father also thought the *recuerdo* was beautiful. "Such a frame as I will make for it," he said.

When the lovely tin frame was finished and the *recuerdo* put inside it, Manuela's mother hung it on the wall for everyone to see.

"Look!" Manuela said, holding the American doll up before it. "It is yourself, a *recuerdo* in honor of my happiest birthday."

WHAT HAPPENED?

Manuela's birthday was wonderful. Her family gave her one thing she didn't expect. It was small, black, and shaggy. What was it?

Manuela's friends did something nice for her, too. What did they do?

The American visitors were very good to her. They made something for her of cloth and wool and ribbon. They even made her a *recuerdo*. What were these fine gifts?

THINK IT OVER

Manuela's family and friends did special things for birthdays. Maybe your family does special things, too. What do you do on birthdays?

265

LUCKY PIERRE

Lorraine and Jerrold Beim

In far-away Brittany there lived a very happy family. They were Mama, Papa, Grandmother, and six children. They all lived in a stone house near the sea.

Whenever visitors came to the house, Mama made her boys and girls stand in a row. "This is Yvon and this is Yvette," she said. "This is Sylvestre and this is Colette. This is Gaos and this is — But where is Pierre?" she cried. Because where there should have been another boy there was no one at all!

"Oh, that Pierre!" the children answered. "He's out in the garden looking for things." Mama went into the garden and there was Pierre under the box tree. "I'm lucky — look what I found!" he called to Mama. "A big fat snail!"

Pierre was always busy looking for things. When the children came down to breakfast in the morning Papa asked, "But where is Pierre?" "Oh, that Pierre!" the children answered. "He's upstairs looking for things." Papa went upstairs and there was Pierre under the bed. "I'm lucky — look what I found!" he called to Papa. "A big shiny pin!"

Pierre's Papa was a fisherman. He went out in his sailboat every day to catch sardines. The boat was called *The Little Marine.* Yvon and Yvette, Sylvestre, Colette, and Gaos carried Papa's fish net to the boat for him. But where was Pierre?

Pierre was 'way down the street looking for things! "Look what I found!" He came running to Papa. "A big old fishhook!" . . .

One morning Pierre looked especially hard for

267

things because the next day was Mama's birthday. He wanted to find her a nice present. How the children laughed. "Mama wants a new lace cap to wear on her head," they said. "And you'll never find that!"

And then Yvon had an idea. "Papa isn't fishing today because he went to visit a friend. Why don't we take the boat and catch some sardines to sell. Then we can buy Mama a beautiful new lace cap." "Oh, yes! That's a wonderful idea!" the children cried, and they danced around Yvon.

That is, they all danced except Pierre. He was busy looking for things. And by the time he finished, the children were running to the boat with Papa's fish net. "Wait for me! Wait for me!" Pierre ran after them. "We haven't time to wait for you!" they called back. "You're too busy looking for things." "But I just found a piece of rope," Pierre said. "Who wants an old piece of rope?" They laughed and hurried on.

Down to the quay they ran, where *The Little Marine* was tied, Yvon and Yvette, Sylvestre, Colette, and Gaos, carrying the fish net with them. "Wait for me! Wait for me!" Pierre ran after them. "We haven't time to wait for you," they said. "You're too busy looking for things." "But I just found a little pail," Pierre said. "Who wants an old pail?" They laughed and hurried into the boat.

Poor Pierre! He got to the boat just in time, though he stopped to pick up a fisherman's needle he found. "Who wants an old fisherman's needle?" the children laughed. "And hurry or we'll go without you!" Pierre ran down the steps and into the boat.

Yvon and Yvette pulled up the sail.

Sylvestre and Colette untied the boat from the quay and then *The Little Marine* sailed out to sea.

The Little Marine sailed and sailed, and when it was far enough away from shore the children lowered the fish net into the sea just as they had seen Papa do. "And now we have to wait for the sardines to swim into the net," Yvon said.

But then a terrible thing happened. The sky began to grow dark and the rain began to fall. A great wind blew up and it blew and blew. It blew so hard that it broke the rope that held the sail.

"Oh, dear, oh, dear, what shall we do?" Yvon and Yvette, Sylvestre, Colette, and Gaos cried. They tried to tie the rope together, but it was too short. "If only we had a piece of strong rope to add to this one!"

"I have a piece of strong rope," Pierre said.

They looked around and there was Pierre with a piece of rope he had found. "How wonderful!" the children cried, and they fixed the sail.

But then the rain came down, harder and harder, and it began to fill the boat. "Oh, dear, oh, dear, what shall we do?" Yvon and Yvette, Sylvestre, Colette, and Gaos cried. "If only we had something to bail out the water!"

"I have a pail," Pierre said. They looked around and there was Pierre with the little pail he had found. "How wonderful!" the children cried, and they bailed out the water with the little pail.

And then the storm ended and the sun came out. "Our net must be full of sardines by now," Yvon and Yvette, Sylvestre, Colette, and Gaos cried, and they pulled up the net. And you never saw such disappointed faces because — there wasn't a single sardine in the net!

"Oh, dear, oh, dear!" Yvon and Yvette, Sylvestre, Colette, and Gaos cried. "There's a hole in the

net as big as a fist and the sardines can swim right through it. If only we had a fisherman's needle to mend it." "I have a fisherman's needle," Pierre said, and he gave them the one he had found. "How wonderful!" the children cried, and Yvette mended the net.

Down went the net into the sea again. And when they pulled it up it was filled with hundreds and thousands of silvery sardines! Then they sailed back to the quay with their catch.

"How much do you want for your sardines?" asked the man at the quay. "Enough to buy our mother a beautiful lace cap for her birthday," the children answered. "Sold!" the man said, and he bought all their sardines.

Down the street the children ran to the shop that sold lace caps. They picked out a beautiful one for Mama, and then they hurried home.

"Children! Children! Where have you been?" Mama asked. "We were fishing for sardines!" Yvon cried.

"The sail broke, but Lucky Pierre found a piece of rope to fix it," Yvette said. "The rain filled the boat with water, but Lucky Pierre found a pail to bail it out," Sylvestre said.

"The net had a hole in it, but Lucky Pierre found a fisherman's needle to mend it," Colette said. "If it hadn't been for Pierre we couldn't have bought you a birthday present," Gaos said.

WHAT HAPPENED?

Pierre really was lucky. He was always finding things. He found a pin. He found a fishhook. What else did he find?

The other children laughed at Pierre. It was silly to keep those things. They were of no use. But the other children were wrong. How did Pierre use the things he found?

THINK IT OVER

Pierre and the other children found a way to get Mama a birthday present. Boys and girls like to get presents for their fathers and mothers. They like to buy things with money they save. They like to make things all by themselves. Have you ever given your father or mother a present without anybody's help? What did you do?

YOUR PICTURE DICTIONARY

A

acorn

(a'corn) the seed of an oak tree
The squirrel ate an *acorn*.

ain't

an old-fashioned way of saying "am not"
We do not use the word "ain't" today.

apartment

(a part'ment) a set of rooms where people live,
often in a city
There is more than one *apartment* in an
apartment house.

axle

the bar or rod which holds a wheel
and lets it turn
Every wheel is fastened to an *axle*.

B

barge

a flat-bottomed boat usually
pushed by another boat
You often see a *barge* in the harbor.

box tree

a small evergreen tree
The *box tree* stays green all winter.

burro

(bur'ro) a small donkey
One of Manuela's presents
was a *burro*.

C

canvas

(can'vas) strong cloth used to make tents
and to cover wagons
Sails on boats are often made of *canvas*.

chipmunk

(chip'munk) a small animal with
stripes down its back
The stripes on a *chipmunk* are
black and white.

274

cinder

(cin′der) a partly burned piece of something
The toast was burned to a *cinder*.

clutched

held tightly
Crossing the street, Daddy *clutched* Susie's hand.

Conestoga wagon

(con es to′ga) a big wagon covered with canvas and used by people long ago when they traveled to far places
Stevie's friend went to Indiana in a *Conestoga wagon*.

corral

(cor ral′) a pen on a ranch where cattle or horses are kept
The horses were in the *corral*.

courtyard

(court′yard) a yard outside a palace or other big building which has walls or high bushes around it
The princess walked in the *courtyard*.

creak

a loud squeak
His shoes would *creak* when he walked.

crotchety

(crotch'e ty) cross or fussy
A person is sometimes *crotchety*
when he is sick.

D

disturb

(dis turb') to bother
Noise might *disturb* a sick person.

doubt

not be sure
I *doubt* that I can do the work.

E

elegant

(el'e gant) very fine
The dress was *elegant*.

elm

a tall tree, rather flat at the top
and good to use as a shade tree
An *elm* tree has branches that spread out wide.

especially

(es pe'cial ly) mostly
We liked all the food, but we *especially* liked
the cake.

276

eyeglasses

(eye'glas ses) glasses to wear so that you can
see better

Many people wear *eyeglasses*.

F

fir

a kind of evergreen tree
Our Christmas tree was a *fir* tree.

firmly

(firm'ly) not to be shaken off or moved
His mother held him *firmly* by the arm.

flageolet

(flag e o let') a musical instrument
made of wood. It has holes in each
side and when these holes are covered
with the fingers, different sounds
can be made.

A *flageolet* is another name for a flute.

flushed

blushed; turned red in color
John *flushed* when the teacher
asked him to read his poem.

277

fortunate

(for'tu nate) lucky

We are *fortunate* to live in a happy town.

G

giraffe

(gi raffe') a large animal with a long neck

A *giraffe* is yellow with large black spots.

gleefully

(glee'ful ly) happily

Ann danced *gleefully* around the room.

H

hack

a carriage drawn by horses

In olden days a *hack* took the place of a taxi.

halfway

half of the way

Father said Don could walk *halfway* downtown.

heave

to lift with great difficulty
They tried to *heave* the rock
out of the garden.

hinge

the joint by which a door or a lid opens
The top of a trunk opens because it is
on a *hinge*.

I

invented

(in vent'ed) made up something new
Someone *invented* a game for the boys and
girls.

instrument

(in'stru ment) that which is used by someone
in order to do something
Each of these things is an *instrument*.

J

jug

a pitcher with a small opening and a handle
Grandma poured milk from the *jug*.

279

K

kerchief

(ker′chief) a piece of cloth
tied over the head

She wore a *kerchief* to keep her ears warm.

kitchen

(kitch′en) the room in which
food is cooked

We could smell something good as
soon as we went into the *kitchen*.

L

lather

(lath′er) foam

Some soap makes a good *lather*.

lickety-split

(lick′e ty) very fast

The boy ran *lickety-split* down the hill.

M

maltese

(mal tese′) a blue-gray cat

The *maltese* cat had a red
ribbon around its neck.

280

marine

(ma rine') having to do with the sea

A whale is a *marine* animal.

mashed

crushed

Mother *mashed* the potatoes for supper.

meanwhile

(mean'while) at the same time

John went to the store. *Meanwhile* we started
to get supper.

mince

a food made of apples, spices, raisins, and
other things

We had *mince* pie for Thanksgiving dinner.

moped

looked sad

Sally *moped* when she broke her doll.

motion

(mo'tion) movement

The policeman made a
motion for us to stop.

N

nope

an old word for "no"

We do not use the word "nope" today.

O

oxen

> (ox'en) cattle which are used
> to help with hard work
> The *oxen* pulled the plow.

outline

> (out'line) the outside line which
> shows the shape of something
> This is the *outline* of a house.

P

parlor

> (par'lor) a living room
> The family sat in the
> *parlor* after dinner.

patiently

> (pa'tient ly) quietly and peacefully
> Jim waited *patiently* for his father.

paused

> stopped for a short time
> The car *paused* before turning the corner.

peer

> to look closely at something
> I like to *peer* at the birds
> outside my window.

prowl

> to wander around
> A dog likes to *prowl* at night.

Q

quay

> a landing place for boats
> The word *quay* sounds like
> the word *key*.

R

radiator

> (ra'di a tor) metal pipes which
> give off heat into a room
> The *radiator* in our school is warm.

refrigerator

> (re frig'er a tor) a box that keeps
> food cold
> We keep milk in our *refrigerator*.

283

remarkable

(re mark'a ble) very good; worth looking at
Tommy drew a *remarkable* picture.

roundup

(round'up) bringing cattle together in one place
Danny wanted to see a *roundup* on the ranch.

ruined

spoiled
The dress was *ruined* when it was torn.

S

sandals

(san'dals) flat, open shoes with
the tops made of straps
Children often wear *sandals* in the summer.

sardine

(sar dine') a very small fish
Kate likes to eat *sardines*.

saucer

(sau'cer) a dish to put under a cup
Mother got out a cup and *saucer* for her coffee.

scampered

ran fast
The dog *scampered* out the door.

shrieking

(shriek'ing) screaming or calling loudly
The children were *shrieking* with joy.

slender

(slen'der) thin
My aunt is very *slender*.

spied

saw or caught sight of
I *spied* him when he tried to enter the house.

steeple

(stee'ple) the tall, thin part of a
church that points toward the sky
The *steeple* on our church is
painted with gold paint.

stirrup

(stir'rup) the part hanging
from a saddle where the
rider puts his foot
Johnny's foot did not reach the *stirrup*.

suggested

(sug ges'ted) helped someone else to think of
something
He *suggested* we play baseball.

285

T

thorn

    the sharp pointed part of a
rose stem or of some other plant
    A *thorn* can stick into your hand and
make it hurt.

tile

    a block of clay or stone used to
cover floors and walls
    Our sun porch has a *tile* floor.

U

upright

    (up'right) standing up straight
    The fence was *upright* when we left yesterday.

V

vain

    proud
    The girl was very *vain* about her long hair.

286

violin

(vi o lin') a musical instrument
A *violin* has strings and is
played with a bow.

W

wailed

cried loudly in a sad way
The wind *wailed* through the trees.

wisps

small pieces
The dog had *wisps* of hay in his fur.

Y

young'un

(young'un) a child; a young one
"Young'un" is an old-fashioned word.

Z

zebra

(ze'bra) an animal that is covered
with black and white stripes
Except for his stripes, a *zebra*
looks almost like a horse.

287

A NOTE TO THE TEACHER

The stories in this book have been used successfully with third grade pupils. Some of the stories are "easy reading"; some contain more advanced vocabulary. The original literary quality has been carefully preserved in all the selections. The picture dictionary at the end of the book is designed as a help for the new words introduced in some of the stories. Every child will thus have his own illustrated book to develop beginning dictionary skills.

Study material following most of the stories has a three-fold purpose: (1) to test reading comprehension and ability to follow sequence of events (2) to lead toward independent thinking on the part of the pupil and (3) to offer opportunity for personal guidance in ethics and behavior.

The section called "Children's Theater" provides opportunity for playmaking and creative dramatics, in addition to the reading and acting out of plays printed in the chapter. Activities introduced here may be carried on throughout the year in connection with stories in other units.

The editors of STORY CARNIVAL offer this book to the pupil and to the teacher with the highest confidence in its ability to stimulate and enrich the young, developing mind.